"How could you seriously think that I would marry you?" he demanded with incredulous bite.

"Naturally I can understand why you would prefer that option. The divorce settlement would be worth millions, and we both know that although you hide it well, there's nothing you wouldn't do for that amount of money!"

Barely able to credit that she was having such a conversation with Valente, Caroline fixed affronted gray eyes on him. "I thought prenuptial agreements dealt with that sort of threat these days. I know you don't believe it, but I don't want your wretched money—"

"There's no way I would stoop to the level of marrying you!" Valente spat out the words with disdainful emphasis. "You're a lying, deceitful, mercenary little witch. Get the idea of marriage right out of your head now."

Caroline kept her head high. "I'm afraid it's the only option I could accept."

"But what would I get out of it, apart from a sense of self-sacrifice?" he asked with unconcealed scorn, outraged by her cheek in even suggesting that idea when she had stood him up ___ earlier.

"Then accept that I will nev ___ Valente. Evidently we've rea ___ her chin, Caroline opened t ___ out onto the landing with as much dignity as she could muster.

"I would want a child...."

All about the author...
Lynne Graham

Of Irish/Scottish parentage, **LYNNE GRAHAM** has lived in Northern Ireland all her life. She has one brother. She grew up in a seaside village and now lives in a country house surrounded by a woodland garden, which is wonderfully private.

Lynne first met her husband when she was fourteen. They married after she completed a degree at Edinburgh University. Lynne wrote her first book at fifteen, and it was rejected everywhere. She started writing again when she was home with her first child. It took several attempts before she sold her first book, and the delight of seeing that book for sale at the local newsagents has never been forgotten.

Lynne always wanted a large family, and she now has five children. Her eldest, her only natural child, is in her twenties and is a university graduate. Her other children, who are every bit as dear to her heart, are adopted: two from Sri Lanka and two from Guatemala. In Lynne's home there is a rich and diverse cultural mix, which adds a whole extra dimension of interest and discovery to family life.

The family has two pets. Thomas, a very large and affectionate black cat, bosses the dog and hunts rabbits. The dog is Daisy, an adorable but not very bright West Highland white terrier, who loves being chased by the cat. At night, dog and cat sleep together in front of the kitchen stove.

Lynne loves gardening and cooking, collects everything from old toys to rock specimens and is crazy about every aspect of Christmas.

Lynne Graham

VIRGIN ON HER WEDDING NIGHT

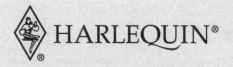

HARLEQUIN®

TORONTO • NEW YORK • LONDON
AMSTERDAM • PARIS • SYDNEY • HAMBURG
STOCKHOLM • ATHENS • TOKYO • MILAN • MADRID
PRAGUE • WARSAW • BUDAPEST • AUCKLAND

If you purchased this book without a cover you should be aware that this book is stolen property. It was reported as "unsold and destroyed" to the publisher, and neither the author nor the publisher has received any payment for this "stripped book."

Recycling programs
for this product may
not exist in your area.

ISBN-13: 978-0-373-23679-4

VIRGIN ON HER WEDDING NIGHT

First North American Publication 2010.

Copyright © 2010 by Lynne Graham.

All rights reserved. Except for use in any review, the reproduction or utilization of this work in whole or in part in any form by any electronic, mechanical or other means, now known or hereafter invented, including xerography, photocopying and recording, or in any information storage or retrieval system, is forbidden without the written permission of the publisher, Harlequin Enterprises Limited, 225 Duncan Mill Road, Don Mills, Ontario M3B 3K9, Canada.

This is a work of fiction. Names, characters, places and incidents are either the product of the author's imagination or are used fictitiously, and any resemblance to actual persons, living or dead, business establishments, events or locales is entirely coincidental.

This edition published by arrangement with Harlequin Books S.A.

For questions and comments about the quality of this book please contact us at Customer_eCare@Harlequin.ca.

® and TM are trademarks of the publisher. Trademarks indicated with ® are registered in the United States Patent and Trademark Office, the Canadian Trade Marks Office and in other countries.

www.eHarlequin.com

Printed in U.S.A.

VIRGIN ON HER
WEDDING NIGHT

CHAPTER ONE

'IT'S all yours, signed, sealed and delivered… the business and the house and land,' the lawyer confirmed.

When Valente Lorenzatto smiled, his enemies took cover. Even his employees had learned to fear the rough passage that might lie ahead. Darkness invariably shadowed that smile and lent it a wolfish quality of threat. While he contemplated the documents set before him, the set of his wide, sensual mouth gave his breathtakingly handsome face a distinctly chilling quality. 'Excellent work, Umberto.'

'It is your own work,' the older man pointed out. 'Your acquisition plan was a triumph.'

Umberto would have given more than his annual bonus, however, to learn exactly *why* his fabulously wealthy employer had devoted so much time and energy to the planned downfall and purchase of an English transport firm and a piece of private property, neither of which appeared to be of sufficient financial or strategic value to justify his interest. Umberto doubted the wild rumour that Valente might once have worked there in the days before his first big deal. It was only after the high point of the latter that the haughty Barbieri family had finally chosen to recognise Valente as Count Ettore Barbieri's illegitimate grandson.

That particular revelation had caused a public sensation, very much in keeping with Valente's colourful lifestyle and his even more spectacular rise to prominence with a series of bold takeovers. Valente was exceptionally clever, and extraordinarily successful in business, but he was even more renowned for his ruthlessness. The Barbieri clan had been very lucky to find a golden goose like him in the family tree at a time when their fortunes had been in need of restoration. Valente's success in that field had proved to be of little comfort to his long-lost relatives, however, when Old Man Barbieri had begun to idolise his grandchild for his dazzling achievements. The Count had ultimately disinherited his other descendents so that he could leave everything he owned, bar his title, to Valente instead.

That development had provided months of tabloid coverage about Valente, who had been asked to take the family name to qualify for his massive inheritance. And, Valente being Valente—a rebel who did not stand for being told to do anything—had gone to court with the argument that he was very proud of his late mother's unremarkable surname, Lorenzatto, and that it would be an offence to her memory and all she had done for him to discard it. Mothers across Italy had lauded him for his attitude. He had won his case to become one of the most illustrious billionaires in the land, regularly consulted for his opinion by the great and good, with his pronouncements quoted in every part of the media. He was, of course, extremely photogenic and media savvy.

Having dismissed Umberto, and other members of his personal staff, Valente took the air on one of the splendid stone balconies that overlooked the busy thoroughfare of Venice's Grand Canal. The Barbieri family had been hugely shocked when he'd taken the ancient Palazzo Barbieri back to its medieval merchant roots and renovated it to act as his business headquarters, just as it had been originally used in the fourteenth century. He had retained only part of the vast, imposing property for accommodation. Valente was a Venetian born and bred, before he was an Italian, and he had kept faith with his late grandfather, Ettore, in doing what had to be done to preserve the *palazzo* for future generations when money might not be in such liberal supply.

Valente drank his black coffee and savoured the moment for which he'd had to work five long years to bring it about. Now he owned Hales Transport, which had finally been brought to its knees by the toxic effect of Matthew Bailey's fraudulent and incompetent management. Valente had also become the owner of a crumbling old house called Winterwood. It was a deeply personal moment of boundless satisfaction for him. As a rule he was neither a patient man nor a vengeful one. After all, he had not sought revenge on his own family, who had left his ailing mother to work as a maid in order to feed and clothe her son. Indeed, if asked, Valente, who generally lived very much in the present, would have said that acts of revenge were a waste of time, and that it was better to move on and forget the past, for the future should hold a more exciting and worthwhile challenge.

Unhappily, however, Valente deliberated, with a harsh expression etched on his bronzed features, even after five years he had yet to meet a woman who excited him anything like as much as his former English bride-to-be, Caroline Hales, once had. His tiny artist, with her pale hair and mist-coloured eyes, who had wept inconsolably when anyone had been cruel to animals but who had, without apparent hesitation or apology, jilted him at the altar for a richer man from a more socially acceptable background.

Just five short years earlier Valente had been an ordinary working man, a truck driver, who'd worked long hours while struggling to complete a business degree in what time was left over. Life had been tough but good—until he'd made the very great mistake of falling head over heels in love with the daughter of the owner of Hales Transport. And Caro, as her adoring family called her, had played him for a fool from the outset, he acknowledged bitterly. She had strung Matthew Bailey and Valente along. And had, regardless of her claims to love Valente, ultimately married Matthew at a big, showy wedding.

Valente savoured the prospect of extracting punishment for those offences against him. He was no longer poor and powerless. Indeed, it had been the rage and aggression incited by the thought of the woman he loved lying naked and willing in another man's arms which had made Valente so fiercely determined to succeed. Soon, however, Caroline would be lying naked and willing in *his* arms, Valente reflected with a saturnine smile. He could only hope the grieving widow he had seen pictured clad in the unrelieved black of mourning would prove to be worth the effort and expense he had already expended on her behalf.

Still, at least he could ensure that when he peeled off the mourning clothes she was at least dressed to his taste. He unfurled his mobile phone and called the owner of Italy's most exclusive lingerie atelier to put in a special order—a Caroline-sized order, in pastel colours that would enhance her pale skin and dainty curves with the finest materials and trimmings available. Even the thought of her parading her sublimely graceful little body in such flimsy apparel for his entertainment caused a painful tightening in Valente's groin. He reckoned that he was a little too sexually hungry for comfort and coolness. He would pay a visit to his current bedmate, Agnese, before he flew to

England to take possession of his new mistress and everything precious to her.

It was time.

His moment had come.

Valente punched out some numbers on his mobile phone and made the call he had been working towards for five years…

Twenty-four hours before Valente made that phone call, Caroline Bailey, formerly Hales, had been engaged in an increasingly upsetting dialogue with her parents. 'Yes, of course I realised that the firm was in trouble last year! But just when did you mortgage the house?'

'In the autumn. The firm needed capital, and pledging the house as security was the only way we could get a bank loan.' Joe Hales settled his portly frame down heavily into an armchair. 'There's nothing we can do about it now, Caro. We've lost the lot. We couldn't keep up the payments and the house has been repossessed…'

'Why on earth didn't you tell me about this at the time?' Caroline prompted in disbelief.

'It was only a few months since you had buried your husband,' her father reminded her. 'You had enough to cope with.'

'We've only been given two weeks to move

out of our home!' Isabel Hales exclaimed. A small blonde woman in her late sixties, with a tight lack of facial lines and movement that suggested a good deal of surgical enhancement, she was the exact opposite in appearance of her tall, heavily built husband. 'I can't believe it. I knew the business was gone—but our home as well? It's a nightmare!'

Engaged in giving her father's heavy shoulder a comforting squeeze, Caroline resisted the urge to try and comfort her tear-stained mother with a hug. She was a touchy-feely person, and always had been, but her mother was not. While her father had grown up secure as the son of the major employer in the district, her mother had been raised by socially ambitious parents who'd been resentful of their lowly status and lack of money. Isabel was their daughter in every way, with the same aspirations and the same reverence for wealth.

Ill-matched though Joe and Isabel might initially have seemed, the only disappointment in their marriage had proved to be Isabel's infertility. The Haleses had been in their forties by the time they'd adopted Caroline at the age of three. As their only child she had enjoyed an excellent education and a stable home life, and would never have dreamt of voicing the reality that she was much closer to her kind-hearted father than her often sharply critical and pushy mother. In truth she had never shared her adoptive mother's aspirations or interests, and was uncomfortably aware that the opinions she held and the choices she made had dismayed and disappointed both her parents.

'How can we only have two weeks to move out of our home?' Caroline exclaimed, in a voice weakened by incredulity.

Joe shook his balding head wearily. 'We're lucky to get that long. A surveyor viewed the whole place last week and went back to our creditors with an offer. It wasn't a great offer, but the administrators snapped it up. They're only interested in paying off the debts and trying to save jobs. I was relieved they had found a buyer for Hales Transport.'

'But too late to be of any help to us!' Isabel Hales snapped angrily.

'I've lost my father's business,' her husband responded heavily. 'Have you any idea how ashamed that makes me feel? Everything my father worked so hard for and achieved, I've lost.'

Tears washing her eyes at his pained speech, Caroline bit her lip and restrained the urge to lament the fact that her parents had not chosen to confide in her before taking out a loan against their home. She would have warned them not to throw good money after bad. She wondered if her mother, who was profoundly attached to her imposing home and comfortable lifestyle, had put excessive pressure on her father to save the business at all costs. Sadly, sound financial judgement had never been one of her father's talents.

Her father had inherited Hales Transport from his own father, and until recently had never known what it was to worry about money. Her mother's snobbish belief that actively running a transport firm lowered their social standing had prevented Joe from assuming much of a hands-on role in the family business. Instead, urged on by his wife, Joe had hired Giles Sweetman, an excellent general manager, to take care of the firm, and had learned how to play golf and fish. For many years the firm had brought in an excellent income. It had taken just two misfortunes to bring about the current crisis.

First, Giles Sweetman had found another job and left with very little warning, and Caroline's late husband, Matthew, had replaced Giles. Although nobody had yet said it to her face, he had been a disaster in the role. The second blow had been the appearance on the local scene of a rival transport firm, hungry for business. One by one Hales had lost the contracts on which it depended for survival to Bomark Logistics, and reducing its workforce had done nothing to halt that downward slide.

'Two weeks is a ridiculously short amount of time,' Caroline protested. 'Who is the buyer? I'll ask if we can have a bit more time.'

'We're not in a position to ask for anything. We no longer own this house,' her father pointed out wryly. 'I just hope that the buyer of Hales isn't planning to make our remaining workers redundant and sell off the firm's assets to the highest bidders.'

Caroline studied her parents, painfully aware of the march of advancing years and ill-health that made them poor candidates to deal with so much stress and upheaval. Her adoptive father suffered badly from angina, and on bad days her mother's arthritic joints made even a walk across the room a painful challenge. Where on earth would they go without the cosy cocoon of financial security which they had enjoyed for so long? How would they cope and survive?

Winterwood was an enchanting, crumbling old house, built at the turn of the century for a large family with domestic staff. It had always been far too big for her parents, but Isabel Hales had been determined to impress everyone in the neighbourhood with visible evidence of her new status as the wife of a wealthy man. The new owner might well be planning to simply knock down Winterwood and redevelop the site. Even in the midst of more serious issues Caroline experienced a sharp pang at the prospect of her childhood home being razed to the ground and the gardens bulldozed.

'You should never have moved out of Matthew's family home and come back here to live with us,' Isabel Hales told her daughter thinly. 'Now you'll have to come with us, and goodness knows where we'll end up living!'

'I still find it hard to believe that Matthew left you with nothing but debt,' Joe admitted with a shake of his head. 'I thought more of him than that. It's a man's job to ensure that his wife has something to live on when he's gone.'

'Matthew could hardly have expected to die so young.' Caroline made her usual soothing response to comments of that nature; she'd had a lot of practice in keeping the secrets of her unhappy marriage to herself. 'But I do wish he had been willing to buy a house, because then I would at least have had a home for the three of us.'

'The Baileys should have helped you more than they did,' her mother contended bitterly. 'Of course you didn't even have the sense to ask for a financial settlement from them.'

'It wasn't their fault that Matthew didn't take out insurance cover, and they did settle all his debts… And let's not forget that they had a stake in Hales as well, and have also lost a good deal of money,' Caroline reminded the older woman ruefully.

'What does that matter now, when we've lost everything we possess?' Isabel Hales demanded shrilly. 'They've still got their home and their household help. But we've got nothing! My friends have stopped phoning me. Word's got around. Nobody wants to know you when you're broke!'

Caroline compressed her lips and kept quiet. It was an unfortunate fact that her mother's friendships were of the shallow sort that relied on status and money and show for fuel. Stripped of what she had once taken for granted, Isabel had been struck off the guest-lists of the well-to-do and socially prominent. It was sad for a woman of her mother's age to suddenly find out that she had become a social pariah, but there was nothing that could be done about it. The spendthrift days of lavish entertainment, designer clothes and fancy holidays were gone for ever.

That same evening, Caroline got back to work in her studio—a converted outhouse in the courtyard behind her parents' home. There she hammered shaped and soldered silver and precious stones into the jewellery she designed and sold on an internet website. It was pains-taking, delicate work, which required a keen eye and full concentration. While she worked, her elegant seal point Siamese cat, Koko, sat like a sentinel on the bench by her side. When Caroline felt a familiar tightening round her brow she knew that one of the nasty migraines she occasionally suffered from was threatening. Soon afterwards she finished off for the night, tidied up and went up to bed.

Of course by then, even though she'd taken her medication to dull the migraine, she was still too stressed to sleep. Tomorrow she would have to start looking for accommodation, she decided, fighting to stave off a growing sense of panic. Finding somewhere suitable to live would not be easy, because she needed space to work as well. Her jewellery business was currently her family's only means of support, aside from their small state pensions.

'Caro?' The next morning Isabel Hales limped painfully into the kitchen where Caroline was preparing breakfast. 'Do you think Matthew's parents would be willing to give us a loan for your sake?' she asked hopefully

Caroline went pale and tensed. 'I don't think so. Settling Matthew's debts was a matter of pride to them. But they're not the type to splash out their cash unless it's likely to benefit them in some way.'

'If only you'd given them a grandchild everything would have been so different,' the older woman replied, in a sharp tone of reproach.

'I know.' Stinging tears burned the back of Caroline's lowered eyes. The Baileys had thrown that omission at her as well while she'd still lived with them. Evidently her failure to produce a child had been her worst flaw as a daughter-in-law, but the Baileys had also insinuated that, had she been a better wife, Matthew would have spent more time at home. She'd had a mad desire to tell them the truth about her marriage, but had mercifully contrived to keep a still tongue in her head. She could not even bear to think about the years she had lost to her unhappy marriage, and nobody would benefit from her talking now about what she had kept hidden for so long. It would only devastate Matthew's parents and shock and upset her own.

'I expect you never thought about the future,' Isabel sighed. 'You were never very practical.'

Caroline's troubled gaze rested on her mother's slight figure as she braced her weight on her walking stick and walked slowly away. The older woman looked horribly small and vulnerable to her daughter. Her parents were already sleeping in a room on the ground floor because of their health problems. Joe was on the waiting list for a coronary bypass. The house really was no longer suitable for them, Caroline conceded ruefully, searching for a silver lining to their situation. But for her parents to be forced out of their home of forty-odd years was a very different matter from making that decision themselves on the grounds of health and common sense.

Koko coiled round Caroline's ankles, loudly crying for attention, and she talked indulgently to her pet while serving breakfast. She skipped eating in her eagerness to write down the urgent list of things to be done that was already unfolding inside her head. But the first list only led into the making of a second. Time, cost and location were crucial factors. At their time of life her parents would not want to move out of the area. It would take ages to track down the right property and save up enough money for a standard rental deposit.

It was fortunate that Caroline adored her adoptive parents. Whilst on one fundamental issue they had once given her what turned out to be very bad advice, they had always sincerely believed that they were putting her best interests first. And now that the elder Haleses were reliant on her financial help, she was happy to repay the debt that she felt she owed them in any way that she could.

The phone rang while she was washing the dishes. 'Can you get that?' she called to her father, who was reading his newspaper in the room next door.

The phone was answered. An instant later Caroline heard an urgent low-voiced exchange between her parents that she couldn't follow and, recognising that they sounded upset, she dried her hands to go and join them

'Caro…will you come here for a moment?' her mother asked stiffly.

The phone was extended to her almost as

though it was an offensive weapon. 'Valente Lorenzatto,' the older woman pronounced between tremulous lips.

Caroline froze like a wax dummy, her face wiped clean of expression. It was a name she had not heard spoken in all the months since she had become a widow, but it still had the power to make her lose colour and shiver as though a cold wind was cutting through her clothes. Valente, whom she had once loved beyond bearing; Valente, whom she had contrived to wrong beyond all possibility of forgiveness. She could not credit that he would have any reason to contact her. Gripping the cordless phone in a damp palm, she walked out into the hall and turned in an aimless circle.

'Hello?' she said, her voice a mere whisper of sound.

'I want to arrange a meeting with you,' Valente breathed in his dark, deep-accented drawl which danced teasing fingers down her taut spinal cord. 'As the new owner of Hales Transport and your family home, I have our mutual interests to discuss.'

It was too shattering a claim for Caroline to accept all at once. 'You own Hales…and the house?' she questioned in stark disbelief.

'It's staggering, isn't it? I made my fortune, as I said I would,' Valente murmured with a surreal cool that mocked her quivering tension. 'Sadly, you backed the wrong horse five years ago.'

Caroline almost laughed out loud—for she had found that out the hard way, and not for reasons he would ever comprehend. What snatched her out of the mesmeric hold of the past was the sight of her parents, staring at her across the hall, evidently having heard what she'd said. Their faces betrayed their profound shock and dismay. The merest mention of Valente Lorenzatto put them on edge, never mind a personal phone call and the suggestion that he might be the new possessor of what had so recently been theirs.

'It can't be true!' Isabel Hales protested in a jagged cry of disbelief.

Caroline very much hoped that it was not true. But she had once, long ago, read about Valente's first big business deal, which had netted him millions on the stock exchange. She had paid a high price for that knowledge, too, when Matthew had found out that she had done a Google search for Valente on their home computer. She had never allowed herself to succumb to that unhealthy streak of curiosity again—not even after she'd become a widow. The past, she believed, was more safely left where it belonged.

'He was only a lorry driver…it's impossible that he could have made so much money!' Joe Hales proclaimed loudly.

'It ought to be impossible,' his wife agreed, tight-mouthed.

Caroline kept the phone crammed hard up against her ear to prevent Valente from over-hearing these embarrassing comments. The fact that her father's father had also been a lorry driver, a self-made man who'd built up his business from nothing by dint of hard work, was never ever mentioned in her home. The older Haleses were ashamed of the humble be-ginnings of their families and had hugely admired Matthew's parents, who had enjoyed private education and were distantly related to titled people. Joe and Isabel Hales were snobs, had always been snobs and would probably be buried as unrepentant snobs, Caroline thought sadly. Valente had never stood on a level playing field with them. He had been judged for what he did and where he came from rather than as the highly intelligent and motivated individual that he was.

Caroline wandered into another room to gain privacy. 'Why do you want to see me?' she asked half under her breath.

'You'll find out when we meet,' Valente delivered with impatience. 'Eleven tomorrow morning, in what used to be your husband's office.'

'But why on earth…?' Her voice faltered to a halt as the connection was cut without warning.

'Let me have that phone, please,' Joe Hales urged his daughter, and she listened while the older man contacted his solicitor to demand the name of the new owner of Hales Transport.

'That Italian boy…' Isabel Hales wore an expression of furious distaste. 'I imagine he's finally found out that you're a widow. It's typical of him—why can't he leave you decently alone?'

'I have no idea.' Caroline could not even be amused by her mother referring to a six-foot-three-inch male of thirty-one years of age as a boy. Valente had never been a boy, she reckoned painfully. He had always had a maturity way beyond his years. She was no more entertained by her mother's ludicrous suggestion that Valente might still cherish a romantic interest in her.

A look of astonishment on his face, her father

replaced the phone. 'Everything that was once ours has been bought up by a very large Italian-based collection of companies known as the Zatto Group,' he proffered dully.

Valente had turned the tables on them, reversing the natural order of things in her mother's opinion. Of all of them, Caroline was the least surprised.

CHAPTER TWO

FOR the meeting, Caroline had chosen to wear her only suit—a tailored black skirt and jacket teamed with a cream silk shirt. She had bought it to wear for her first sales pitch to the high-end London jewellery store which had been successfully selling her designs for the past year. Since then she had lost weight, and the fit was now more than a little loose on her. With her hair swept up, and a modest smattering of make-up to give her the natural colour she lacked after a stressed-out sleepless night, she looked harried when she climbed out of her hatchback car at Hales Transport the next morning.

'Hello, Mrs Bailey,' Jill, one of the receptionists, greeted her, with surprising good cheer for a member of a workforce that had been suffering from mass anxiety over the firm's uncertain future for many weeks. 'Isn't this an exciting day?'

Caroline blinked uncertainly and brushed a straying strand of pale hair back from her too-warm brow. 'Is it?'

'The new boss is flying in. We're becoming part of a big business group that's worth billions. It can only be good news for us,' Jill opined chirpily.

'Don't be so sure of that,' remarked Laura, the senior receptionist, looking up from her computer screen to cast a rueful glance at Caroline. 'Have you never heard of that expression "a new broom"? There's no guarantee that we'll all keep our jobs, or even that this business will still exist six months from now.'

A cold trickle of apprehension rolled down Caroline's taut spine. She was really worried about what might happen to their former employees at Hales Transport. And that concern ran even deeper as she was guiltily conscious that her late husband had taken financial risks but had neglected the day-to-day running of the firm during the last year of his life.

Breathing in deep, she took a seat in the waiting area. 'Let's all hope for the best,' she urged Laura.

'I'm sure you could just go up and wait in the office,' Jill told her innocently. 'It's not as if you don't know your way around.'

Her colleague frowned at that advice. 'I think Mrs Bailey will be more comfortable waiting down here.'

'Yes, I'm fine,' Caroline hastened to declare, her face warming in response to the curious glances she received from a group of employees passing by to mount the stairs. The low-pitched buzz of conversation that broke out among them made her skin heat even more as an anguished surge of self-consciousness gripped her.

Caroline had avoided coming to Hales Transport during the last months of Matthew's life, and in the time since his sudden death in a car crash. The fear that people were talking about her, even laughing at her, had kept her at a distance. Her in-laws and parents had censured her for not attending work-related events with them, but Caroline had no desire to pose as Matthew's martyred widow.

After all, there had to be others who were aware of or had at least suspected her late husband's extra-marital interests. As the effects of his lifestyle had taken a firmer hold Matthew had become considerably less discreet about the double life he'd been leading. All the moments of cringing embarrassment and hurt that Caroline had endured had left their mark on her. She had been a fool—a stupid, blind fool—and a dupe. It was almost impossible for her to recall that Matthew had once been her closest friend, since their marriage had soon put paid to that bond. She suppressed her thoughts, rejecting her deeply unhappy memories

'He's here!' the younger receptionist hissed in excitement when a long dark limousine pulled up outside. Two Mercedes cars arrived simultaneously, and their passengers were disgorged first. A phalanx of men in business suits collected on the steps and parted like the Red Sea for the passage of a tall, powerful figure sporting a heavy cashmere overcoat in spite of the spring sunshine.

'He's even more handsome than in his photos,' Jill sighed dreamily.

The breath caught in Caroline's throat as she focused on the lean, strong face below the swept back, cropped, but defiantly curly hair. Hair that she knew Valente only kept in order with frequent haircuts—hair that had been longer when she'd first known him. And how she had once loved to run her fingers through those black curls. Frozen in her seat, she had literally stopped breathing. Seeing Valente when she had believed that she would never, ever see him again was a surreal experience.

He was an astonishingly handsome man, she conceded in a daze. He had dark, deep eyes that could turn as hotly golden as the heart of the sun, level brows, stunning cheekbones, and an arrogant blade of a nose that would have looked at home on the marble face of a classic Roman statue. He was all her past sins come back to haunt her at once, reminding her of the heartbreak and the fear and the craving that had once torn her apart. In a designer business suit he emanated a sleek elegance and assurance that was totally Italian. Even in jeans and a sweater, she recalled, Valente had had the art of looking as if he had just stepped off a fashion catwalk.

'Caroline,' he murmured, pausing at the foot of the stairs to note her presence in that dark, unforgettable drawl that was inherently sexy. 'Come up to the office. I'll see you straight away.'

Painfully aware of suddenly being the centre of attention as curious heads turned in her direction, Caroline avoided the perceptible chill of his hooded dark gaze and rose upright. His informality had just made it obvious that they had a prior history—one which she hoped nobody else could remember. It was a history

which Valente could only hate her for, she acknowledged unhappily. Crippling guilt twisted
inside her stomach and threatened to overpower
her. She had known he would never forgive her
for what she had done. Nor would he ever recognise the pressure she had buckled under,
squeezed between everybody she loved, trying
to please everyone and ending up by pleasing
no one. He would only despise such weakness.

A skimming appraisal of Caroline's drab,
loose-fitting suit, and of her hair twisted up into
a dreary girlish plait at the back of her head,
gave Valente's handsome mouth a sardonic curl.
He wanted to see her white-gold hair flowing
loose over an outfit that complemented her
slender figure and delicate colouring. Black
gave her all the appeal of a wraith. He wanted
to eradicate every hint of Matthew Bailey's
good-living little widow, who fixed the flowers
in the local church and made jewellery in her
spare time. He wanted so much—and, at that
first moment, even twenty-four hours felt like
too long a wait for fulfilment.

One of his PAs raced ahead of them to throw
open the door of the main office. The room was
familiar to Caroline—a first-class display of
Matthew's love of ultra-modern furniture and

design—though it was out of keeping with the
style of the building and had been created at
ruinous expense.

Valente shrugged off his coat and the PA bore
it away. He turned to look at Caroline, seeing
the sun slant through the window to glitter over
the pale crown of her head. She looked at him
directly, her misty grey eyes wide and dark with
bewilderment and tension. A lusty throb of
sexual awareness infiltrated Valente at groin
level, and roused him so thoroughly that he was
grateful for the concealment of his jacket. He
couldn't wait to give her the lingerie.

Meeting that lingering sensual appraisal head-
on, Caroline felt her body react in a way she had
honestly thought it no longer could. Matthew
had told her that she was useless in bed, and that
she turned him off so much he could not even
stand to share a room with her. He had been very
frank and very cruel. It was ironic, therefore,
that she should now feel her nipples tingle as they
swelled, and a startling kick of heat in her pelvis
in response to a male whom instinct warned her
had it in him to be a great deal more cruel. Her
body, which had inhabited a sort of dead zone for
years, was suddenly reacting again, and coming
alive in a way that unnerved her.

'So, you own everything now,' Caroline remarked brittly, fighting to shut down that physical awareness which shamed and affronted her on every level.

'*Si, piccola mia.*' Drawing level, Valente stared down at her with brooding eyes, noting the rapidity of her breathing while he savoured the pale perfection of her skin, the flickering colour of her eyes and the soft pink invitation of her surprisingly full mouth. That fine profile, the flutter of her soft curling lashes on her cheeks, the nervous tightening of the tiny muscles round her tender mouth spoke of vulnerability and brought out the predator in him—because he knew that she was at heart nothing more than a callous little gold-digger with great acting skills. She was his polar opposite in looks and personality but, regardless, the minute he saw her again he wanted her with a fierce power and impatience that was already disturbing his equilibrium.

'You should have had more faith in me,' Valente continued in the same tone of laidback cool, his rock-hard self-discipline controlling him.

Caroline snatched in a sharp breath. 'What do you want me to say? That I'm sorry? I am—'

'I don't want an apology.' Valente's interruption cut like a slashing knife through her softer voice. He was dangerously still, his big, powerful frame taut with pent-up energy and anger as he watched her. Her face was as devoid of emotion as a doll's, only her wide eyes revealing her anxiety. She was different; she had changed, he registered with a frown, had become a woman who no longer wore her every feeling on her face. Presumably she had finally grown out of being the very much indulged daughter of older parents and had learned to stand on her own feet. Such very small feet too, he reflected, sheathed in no-nonsense flat pumps that had all the sex appeal of carpet slippers. He decided then and there that he would make a bonfire of her entire wardrobe.

'I don't understand why you would want everything that used to belong to my family,' Caroline admitted.

'Don't be so modest,' Valente chided.

Caroline stood poker-straight, making the most of her every diminutive inch of height. 'I'm not being modest. I don't even know why you asked me to meet you here.'

'That's simple,' Valente murmured softly. 'I hoped we could come to a civil agreement which would give each of us what we most want. I'll go first on that issue—I want you in my bed.'

Caroline was so astonished by that statement that she opened her mouth and hastily shut it again. 'Is this your idea of a joke?' she enquired curtly.

'I work hard and I play hard. I take my sex-life too seriously to joke about it. Unfortunately I haven't got much more time to give you this morning. There are too many other claims on my attention,' he imparted smoothly. 'But naturally I'm aware that you and your parents are having a very hard time at present.'

'Yes.' Caroline gave that jerky confirmation still unnerved by his previous crack, wondering what on earth she would do if he was to make her some outrageous offer in that line. Tell him that she was the last woman in the world capable of fulfilling a man's expectations in the bedroom? That it was a horrible black joke to even consider her in that guise?

'Obviously there's a great deal I could do to alleviate your current situation.' Dark lashes dipping low on his stunning gaze, Valente purred that assurance. 'But you would have to persuade me that it would be worth my while.'

'I don't think I'm up to persuading you to do

anything—nor do I follow your meaning,' Caroline told him stiltedly

'I still want the wedding night you denied me…'

Caroline was jolted into reaction by that blunt reminder. 'But we didn't get married!'

'Precisely…but that fact didn't stop me wanting you,' Valente countered. 'And you should be aware of the fact that the answer you give me now will impact on the lives of everyone connected with this business.'

Her fine brows drew together in a frown of consternation. 'The answer to *what* question?' she prompted in frustration.

Valente shook his arrogant dark head. 'I've already told you what I want.'

'Sex?' Caroline shook her fair head in sincere wonderment over so preposterous a suggestion. He was young, movie-star handsome and rich, and any number of beautiful, sophisticated women would offer him no-strings-attached sex without hesitation. Why on earth should he decide to approach *her*?

'I will be plain. I want you as my mistress.'

A rather shrill laugh was finally wrenched from Caroline. She knew she sounded hysterical and, fearful of him, realising just how out of her depth she was feeling, she walked hurriedly over to the window that overlooked the car park. That pedestrian view helped steady her nerves. How could he possibly want her as his mistress? It was true that five years earlier Valente had been hot for her. As she remembered the sexual urgency which she had withstood out of fear of making that final commitment to him a sharp little pang of reaction pierced low in her pelvis. Now, as then, she wondered if he would have swiftly lost interest had she slept with him. Would she have been as inadequate with him as she had been with Matthew? She scolded herself for that meaningless question, for it was far too late now to change anything. And, what was more, she didn't want to remember her sexless marriage—even less did she want to think about it or beat herself up about it.

'You really would be very disappointed if I agreed,' Caroline replied shakily. 'I just don't have what it takes to meet the demands of a role like that. Some women are into sex, some women aren't. I'm very much in the second category.'

Lean strong hands came down on her narrow shoulders and turned her back round to face him. He was very close, and the aromatic scent of his cologne mingled with the faint musky aroma of masculinity almost made her head spin. There was grim amusement now in his hard black-lashed golden eyes. 'No, you're not. You could never disappoint me. Did you disappoint Matthew?'

Reacting to that horribly accurate counter-question, Caroline put up her arms to break free of their connection and took several agitated steps away, spinning back to him to say, 'You're not listening to me, are you? What do I have to say to convince you?'

Exasperated by her skittish retreat when his whole body was humming for closer contact, Valente sent her a level look of warning. 'Doing rather than saying would be more convincing. Come back to my hotel with me and give me a demonstration of your unsuitability.'

Her grey eyes widened to their fullest extent and hardened to glittering steel as her temper erupted. 'What do you think I am? A whore?' she shot back at him in furious condemnation.

'The jury is still out on that one. Let's not overlook the reality that, while you might not be a whore, you *did* sell yourself to the highest bidder five years ago,' Valente derided without hesitation.

Caroline turned pale as milk at that come-back. 'That's not how it was—'

'Why would I want to know how it was now?' Valente interposed very drily. 'If you must know I'm grateful I was saved from making the mistake of marrying you. When I do take a wife, I don't want a gold-digger for the role.'

'How dare you?' Caroline lashed back at him, colour washing her cheekbones as his insults drove her indignation to even greater heights. 'That's not why I married Matthew! Money had nothing to do with it.'

'What about social status?' Valente quipped, shrugging back his shirt-cuff to glance at his watch. 'I can only give you two more minutes. You're wasting your breath, arguing with me. I know what you are and, strange as it may seem, no insult was intended. After all, I'm willing to pay a great deal of money for the privilege of having you in my bed.'

'You can't buy me…'

Valente rested cold dark eyes on her, his lack of conviction coolly emphasising his contempt. 'Can I not? If you say no, I will close down this firm and put everyone out of work. I will also make no attempt to ease your parents' plight…'

Reeling in shock from that deeply disturbing

caveat, Caroline parted pale lips. 'That would be utterly immoral and unjust—'

'On the other hand, if you say yes to my proposition, I will invest in this business and ensure it prospers for many years to come,' Valente informed her dulcetly. 'I will also allow your parents to remain at Winterwood at my expense.'

'That's an impossible, absolutely disgusting choice to give me!' Caroline gasped in growing disbelief. 'You're trying to blackmail me!'

'Am I?' Valente rested brilliant dark impenitent eyes on her flushed and furious face. 'It depends what you want, doesn't it? Come to me on my terms and you will be treated well and want for nothing that your heart desires. It's a very generous offer from a man who has no reason to like you, much less respect you.'

'If you neither like nor respect me, you can't possibly want me that much,' she threw back in breathless defiance.

His dark gaze burned scorching gold. 'But I do. There's no accounting for taste.'

Before she could guess his intention he had closed a hand over hers. While she stiffened, every muscle seizing taut, he proceeded to tug her across the space that separated them with cool determination. In a movement she could no more have prevented than she could have stopped breathing, Caroline broke violently free of his hold and fell back for support against the wall.

'What the hell is the matter with you?' Valente demanded in a raw undertone, watching her breathe in and out with the rapidity and heaving bosom of a woman on the edge of panic. 'Did you think that I was about to attack you?'

Caroline was mortified by her knee-jerk reaction, and suddenly terrified that he might guess she was something less then the average woman when it came to intimacy. 'Of course not…I'm s-sorry,' she stammered. 'It's just been a long time since anyone touched me.'

Valente studied her, sensing something more. She was very tense and jumpy—a far cry from the calm young woman of twenty-one whom he recalled. Still waters ran deep. He had never wanted to know what her marriage was like, that being a can of worms that he preferred to leave firmly closed. But he knew enough to suspect that marriage to her childhood sweetheart had proved to be no picnic for her: Bailey had mismanaged the business, spent a fortune he didn't have on luxury goods and left his wife penniless. He had also been rumoured to have slept with other women.

'Really, I don't know what came over me,' Caroline babbled, moving away from the wall, smoothing down her skirt and even trying to pitch a faint smile on to her strained mouth. Her pride had come to her rescue. She could not bear the idea that he might suspect just what an oddity she was in comparison to other women. That was her secret shame alone. How else could she feel about herself when she was still a virgin after almost four years of marriage? It was not a truth, however, that she was prepared to share.

'No?' Quite deliberately Valente strolled forward, keen dark golden eyes nailed to her delicate features. He closed an arrogant hand over hers in an unexpected rerun of events and she snatched in a startled breath, stiffening again. He drew her closer and angled down his proud dark head to taste her mouth, with a tender touch and skill that made her head swim as dismay collided with surprise. Instead of freezing, as fear and revulsion rippled through her to make her feel nauseous, she stayed still, wondering, waiting, helplessly curious.

She had forgotten what it was like to be kissed by Valente. His breath fanned her cheek and her knees turned to jelly. The citrus aroma of his cologne made her tummy perform a somersault and she trembled, every nerve-ending screaming in quivering alert. He didn't touch her body, made no attempt to hold her, and that sense of retaining the freedom to move strengthened and soothed her. His expert mouth was smooth as silk on hers, searching and uniquely sensual, to the extent that she leant forward to deepen the connection. He captured her lips then, and parted them with feathery delicacy, pausing to suckle at her full lower lip with lethal eroticism before slickly invading the moist, responsive space beyond. Beneath her clothing her nipples peaked into straining prominence, and a small sound came from low in her throat.

As that revealing gasp escaped her, Valente lifted his handsome head, narrowed dark eyes executing an almost clinical inspection of her bemused expression. He stepped back from her. She might be tense, she might be nervous, but she was still hot and ready for him, he reflected with considerable satisfaction. He was so aroused by the scent and the taste of her that with very little encouragement he would have settled her on to the desk behind him and eased himself into the silky welcome of her body without further ado. The very thought of having hot casual sex with Caroline whenever and wherever he wanted excited him.

'Time's up, *piccola mia*,' he told her softly as an urgent knock sounded on the door.

As taut as a bowstring, Caroline again skimmed damp palms down over her skirt. Her brain was working at the frantic speed of fright. 'You can't mean what you just said—what you… er…suggested,' she framed unevenly.

'Unlike you, I'm very into sex,' Valente confided deadpan, watching colour surge up below her skin while her delicate bone structure froze beneath it. He marvelled that even after several years of marriage to a boor she could still be so prudish. But then, he reflected lazily, her attitude told him even more. Evidently Bailey had botched his role in the bedroom. That was a little piece of knowledge that Valente, who had never ever failed to please a woman, prized more than any other.

The door opened and a young man addressed him in an apologetic rush. Valente moved a silencing hand. 'Abramo, I'm aware that I'm running late. Show Mrs Bailey back to her car—'

'That's not necessary,' Caroline protested. 'We have to talk about what you said right now—'

Valente turned cold dark eyes on her. 'What would we talk about? There's no room for negotiation. I'll see you this afternoon at Winterwood.'

'At…Winterwood? 'Caroline exclaimed in horror.

'It is my property. I'll see you at four for a guided tour.'

Caroline was appalled.

Valente dealt her a slashing smile that had the effect of making her back away from him. 'And warn the family that I won't be using the tradesman's entrance, *piccola mia.*'

'Mrs Bailey?' the PA prompted, holding the door invitingly wide for her exit.

Seeing that she had no other choice, Caroline left the office. She was trembling with rage. She never swore, but she wanted to hurl curses at Valente. She yearned for the physical strength to grab him by the lapels of his fancy suit and slam him up against the wall to make him listen to her!

Sadly, Valente was evidently driven by too powerful a compulsion for revenge to award her a more generous hearing. Five years ago she had jilted him at the altar. Her misplaced trust in another person and her illness had together plunged Valente into the humiliating position of a bridegroom left standing by his bride.

Circumstances had left her unable to ensure that he was forewarned of her change of heart before he reached the church. Although Valente had been informed of those mitigating factors after the event, it was very plain that he still blamed her for what he had undergone that day. After all, she still blamed herself, recognising the appalling blow that her no-show must have dealt Valente's ferocious pride. He had fought for her and lost, and his iron will could not accept defeat.

Even in the act of driving back home Caroline shivered. Valente had grown up fighting poverty and fighting for everything he'd ever wanted. That gritty raw-edged struggle for survival, the losses and slights he had endured, had ignited a primitive streak of dark cruelty and strength in him that had intimidated Caroline when she'd first known him. He'd had little time for her refined attitudes, and he'd downright despised her continuing allegiance to her parents, who had done everything they could to break up his relationship with her.

'If you really love me, you can overcome anything,' Valente had told her five years earlier.

He had expected so much from her, Caroline acknowledged painfully. But she had been raised too gently to have his power and his conviction, his ability to reject and ignore the feelings of those who did not share his objectives.

As her emotions shifted back and forth between past and present, memories that Caroline had long suppressed came floating back to the surface of her mind.

The summer after she'd completed her apprenticeship with a jewellery designer she had longed for the capital to set up her own business. That she'd been a child with aspirations to build her own business had been a severe disappointment to the Hales, who had hoped for a much more feminine and frivolous daughter, eager to enjoy the local social scene and find a suitable husband. Determined not to ask her parents for their financial help when they disapproved of her ambitions, Caroline had taken a temporary office job at Hales, so that she could save up the money she needed to start her company. Ironically that decision had shaken Joe and Isabel even more, for they had considered the transport firm too crude a working environment for their much-adored child.

Just two days after she'd started work in the office where administration was handled, Caroline had looked up and seen Valente for the first time. The liquid flow of his accented English had initially attracted her attention, but it had been her first mesmerising glimpse of his lean dark face which had made her stare. No words could ever hope to describe the intense sense of recognition and fascination that drop-dead beautiful face of his had fired her with. Ignoring her colleague, who had been trying to flirt with him, Valente had skimmed a glance over Caroline, his ebony-lashed eyes flaring hot gold in a lengthy appraisal. In the same moment Caroline had been lost to all reason, ensnared by his stunning gaze. It hadn't mattered who or what he was. He had taken her prisoner with a single glance, and she would have followed him to the ends of the earth on the strength of it.

'And you are…?' Valente had murmured, poised by her desk.

'Caroline—'

'The boss's daughter…our poor little rich girl!' one of the other drivers had spelt out in warning, causing the warm blood of embarrassment to rise beneath her fair skin.

'I'll see you later, Caroline,' Valente had breathed silkily. Just the timbre of his rich dark drawl had made her skin come up in goosebumps.

The afternoon had dragged while she'd pictured that lean dark face over and over again, recalling his high masculine cheekbones, narrow-bladed nose and wide, sensual mouth, wondering dizzily what it was about that precise arrangement of features that had made it almost impossible for her to look away from him again. Even though she'd been twenty-one years old, she'd fallen for Valente Lorenzatto with the speed and wholehearted enthusiasm of a schoolgirl.

In those days she had been no more experienced than an innocent schoolgirl, either. The safe cocoon of her cushioned upbringing had made her something of a misfit at art college. The aggressive sexual demands of the boys she'd met then had put her off anything more than the most casual dating. When she'd needed a partner for more formal occasions she'd invited Matthew Bailey—the boy next door and her closest friend. An introvert and shy, and cautious with strangers, she had already been carrying a load of guilt for disappointing her parents. In going for a college education Caroline had defied the wishes of the parents she loved for the first time…Valente had been the second and a by far more serious demonstration of her growing need for the freedom to act as an individual in her own right...

Refusing to agonise over the situation with Valente now, Caroline told herself that he just could not be serious, and to keep herself busy did the weekly shopping before returning home. There she found a note from her mother on the kitchen board, reminding her that her father had a hospital appointment that afternoon. Her parents had already left. Groaning, because she had forgotten about the arrangement, Caroline stowed away the groceries. By that stage her ability to shut out her recollection of Valente's threat to close down Hales Transport was wearing dangerously thin.

Over two hundred people would lose their jobs, not to mention the knock-on effect on other neighbourhood businesses. Another local firm had gone bust several years earlier and the whole community had suffered a great deal. She knew that the stress of unemployment and the loss of a steady income could break up marriages and shatter families. To allow that to happen to others when she had been offered an alternative—no matter how outrageous—was a huge responsibility that rested on her shoulders alone.

And who more justly deserved that responsibility? Caroline asked herself angrily. Matt had made little effort to reduce his spending when Hales had lost contracts to Bomark Logistics. Instead, he'd bought a very expensive new company car and run up huge bills entertaining prospective clients, whom she suspected had never really existed. She had been no friend to the family business while she'd loyally kept her mouth shut about her husband's failings. Guilt cut her deep. Matthew's behaviour had been a deep source of shame to her, yet she had shrunk from distressing her parents or his with the news that Matthew was not to be trusted with the future of an ailing business. There again, nobody would have wanted to hear, and nor would any of them have listened to her or valued her opinion, she reflected heavily. Sexism had run through both sides of the family like a contagious disease. And Matthew had been idolised by his parents, who'd believed he was the keenest and cleverest businessman around.

Valente said he wanted sex from her, but how could she possibly still appeal to him to that degree? No, what he really wanted, Caroline decided ruefully, was revenge. And if by letting him have that revenge she could protect her parents from being evicted from their home and she save almost two hundred and fifty jobs at Hales, did she really have the right to refuse him?

Goodness, was she *actually* contemplating a new lifestyle as Valente Lorenzatto's mistress?

A pained laugh was wrenched from her compressed lips. Valente would soon realise that he had struck a very bad bargain. She felt sick at the very idea of such a humiliation, but if that was what it would take to satisfy his desire for retribution could she really stand back and let so many other people suffer? It was her fault that Valente was angry and bitter, nobody else's. She had let him down.

But how could she even consider surrendering to his demands? If she became intimately involved with Valente it would cause too much distress for her strait-laced parents, who had long believed that only shameless women slept with men they weren't married to. A lurid affair would horrify and humiliate them, and her father's health would never stand up to that upsetting challenge. Nor, in such circumstances, would Joe and Isabel Hale agree to continue living in a house owned and maintained by their daughter's lover. But what if Valente could be persuaded to lower his expectations and settle for a one-night stand which could be kept a secret? She shifted uneasily on her seat, wondering in cringing embarrassment whether he would ask for his money back when she signally failed to please between the sheets.

Such thoughts made her feel sleazy, made her feel like the whore he had suggested she might be, and her pride was already in the dust. But, at the end of the day, a body was just a body, she told herself flatly, and it was highly unlikely that Valente would be violent or abusive. After all, he wanted her to want him, didn't he? To want him so that it would hurt when he dropped her again? Couldn't she pretend, suppress the fear, make a real effort to be normal? Tears burning the back of her eyes, she rammed shut the mental door threatening to open on her painful memories. Matthew would not have sought other lovers had she managed to be a good wife. Hadn't he told her so, times without number? It was a heavy burden for her conscience to carry.

On the other hand, Valente was offering her an indefensibly corrupt arrangement which made her feel that she owed him nothing in terms of honesty. He was playing a cruel game with her. Did she have the nerve to fight for terms which would make an agreement possible?

CHAPTER THREE

CAROLINE was taken aback when not one but three luxury vehicles pulled up outside Winterwood shortly after four that afternoon. She had dimly assumed that Valente would arrive without an entourage. This would make a private chat impossible.

Valente emerged fluidly from his limo, his every movement laced with the predatory grace that was as much a part of him as his ability to breathe. He cut an impressive figure in his supremely elegant dark suit, which accentuated his broad shoulders, lean hips and long, powerful legs. He strode into the entrance hall closely followed by three other men. He already knew to expect the flashy décor, so it was his companions who stared in surprise when they realised that almost everything, from the fake marble pillars to the elaborate furniture, was gilded. It was bad taste central, Valente acknowledged with concealed amusement, the attempt of a nouveau riche family to present a country house in the guise of an historic stately home.

With unblemished cool, Valente introduced Caroline to an architect, a surveyor, and a keen-looking local man she recognised as the owner of a building firm well known for restoring period properties. 'They're here to see the house and get some plans down on paper. It would make more sense if they were allowed to explore at their own pace,' he said.

Caroline was appalled that he was already making plans to alter her parents' home. 'Of course,' she acceded. as if the matter was of no concern to her—because she knew that she had no grounds for interfering.

'Where are your parents?' Valente asked with a frown as his companions took off in different directions to do his bidding. He had expected to renew his acquaintance with the older couple who had in the past slighted him with their distaste, quite unaware that as an illegitimate Barbieri he had been abused by true professionals in that field and had developed a tough skin after enduring much more painful rejections and dismissals. He ran his unimpressed gaze over the faded jeans and the ruffled purple shirt that Caroline now sported. The outfit at least fitted her delicate figure and made her look much younger than her years. The shirt also lent a reflected purple depth to her silvery eyes, while less innocently outlining the rounded, tip-tilted firmness of her small bosom. His even white teeth clenched and his body reacted accordingly to those delectable breasts, even before he noted the tight fit of the denim over the curve of her hips.

Registering that all-over distinctively masculine appraisal, Caroline reddened and felt warm all over, as if her temperature had gone haywire. Valente had always had that effect on her. Unlike many very good-looking men, Valente had never gone through a New Man or metrosexual phase. He was an aggressive alpha male who emanated high-voltage sexuality and potent virility. Women of all ages were always aware when Valente was around. 'My parents are out…my father has a hospital appointment.'

'Their absence should only make life simpler,' Valente remarked. 'Let's get on with this. I have a tight schedule.'

He revealed no interest, indeed his frown merely deepened, as she showed him through to the handsome main reception rooms where her mother had spared no expense in either colour scheme or embellishment. 'Look, you can't possibly want to live here,' she told him sharply. 'I can't believe that you would have sufficient use for this house, or that it could ever be made over in your style.'

'If you were waiting here to welcome me when I arrived for a visit, I could learn to like it. In any case—' a sleek black brow quirked with sardonic cool '—what could you possibly know about how I live now?'

'The designer clothes and the limousines speak for you. This house was never in that class even when it was new!'

'Sniping at me won't drive me away, and nor will it win you favours,' Valente breathed lazily. 'This property belongs to me and I will do as I like with it.'

'But my parents—'

'I don't want to hear another word! I have a hearty contempt for sob stories,' Valente incised with chilling bite. He shifted a lean brown hand in dismissal when she attempted to show him the kitchen quarters, and headed for the main staircase instead. 'Neither of your parents has ever worked a day in their lives, or even had the good sense to cut back on their lifestyle when

their business began going down. I refuse to
see them as victims of anything but their own
self-indulgence.'

Silenced by that harsh condemnation,
Caroline swallowed back the protest that her
parents deserved a little more sympathy
because as their income had dwindled so their
household budget had had to be slashed. All
extras had been shaved away, the housekeeper
and the gardener laid off. Valente was not the
man to give her family sympathy, for there was
too big a difference between their backgrounds.
Caroline had never wanted for anything while
Valente had grown up in poverty with a mother
whose ill-health had killed her by the time he
was eighteen. His tougher experiences had
ensured that only major affliction could ignite
his compassion.

'Even so, your parents did not deserve your
husband's betrayal of their trust,' Valente continued drily with an observation that caused
Caroline to stumble on the stairs.

His hand shot out to steady her and he
stepped behind her to prevent her from falling
backwards. Momentarily, his body braced hers,
with all the heady heat and masculinity of his
powerful frame. She quivered and then tensed,

fighting her awareness of his proximity with all her might.

'What on earth are you implying?' Caroline asked curtly.

'Your late husband was nothing more than a thief, who helped himself to profits even when the business was struggling—'

On the landing, Caroline spun round to face him, agitation and anger colouring her heart-shaped face. 'He may have spent unwisely on some items, but he was not a thief!'

'My auditors and the firm's accountant could tell you otherwise and show you plenty of proof. Your husband set up a dummy business account and he milked it every opportunity he got.'

Her attention resting on the sombre planes of Valente's darkly handsome features, Caroline registered the depth of conviction in his own words and paled. 'Are you sure?'

'Certain. Odd, that, isn't it, *piccola mia*?' Valente remarked softly. 'Your parents thought I would plunge their little princess into a squalid life, and yet it was the golden, public-school-educated boy-next-door who had the criminal streak and the bad habits. He couldn't keep his hands out of the till or off his employees!'

Caroline saw red. Trembling in the grip of fury

and humiliation, she lifted her hand and slapped him—*crack!*—across one proud olive cheekbone. 'Matthew's dead...show some respect!'

'Don't ever dare to hit me like that again.' Eyes black as coals and angrily bright as diamonds, Valente made his warning soft and low and icy.

'You took me by surprise. It won't happen again,' Caroline told him in a rush, shocked at her complete loss of temper and control.

'I have no respect for your late husband...or you, for that matter...because you stayed with him until the bitter end. Yet you knew what he was capable of, didn't you?' he condemned with lethal accuracy. 'I saw your face. You weren't sufficiently shocked to have been ignorant of his greed or his selfishness—'

Still trembling, Caroline moved so that one of the men who had accompanied him into the house could get past her and head down the stairs. 'I didn't know about the account you mentioned,' she admitted in a pained whisper. 'I knew he had been extravagant but I had no idea that he might actually be stealing. Please don't publicise the fact—'

'Even dead, Matthew's sacred and untouchable, is he?' Valente derided in disbelief.

'His parents would never recover from the disgrace if what you've just told me got out. He can't be punished now. Let his family keep their memories of him clean and intact,' she pleaded vehemently.

Valente was outraged by that plea. Did she truly expect him to throw a cloak of respectful concealment over her late husband's fraud? Bailey—the guy who had supplanted Valente in her heart and in her bed?

Caroline read the anger in the clenched set of his fabulous bone structure, and the grim glow of displeasure in his hard dark gaze. A kind of panic threatened what remained of her composure and she shifted her feet restively. This was a meeting she had known she had to get right, but instead it was going badly wrong.

From round the corner drifted the sound of male voices engaged in lively dialogue about where to carve out extra bathroom space in the old house.

Before they could be interrupted, and Valente distracted by them, Caroline reached a sudden decision. She opened the door into the unused master bedroom suite behind her and closed a hand over Valente's sleeve to tug him in there with her. 'We have to talk…'

'What about? I made you a simple proposition,' he declared, with more than a hint of impatience, although he twisted his hand around to catch her fingers in the grip of his. 'This morning you were undecided—'

Caroline leant back against the door to close it. 'I was not undecided. I made it very clear that what you were suggesting was out of the question.'

'Except when I was kissing you,' Valente tossed in lazily, his satisfaction at that recollection patent. His long fingers stroked the sensitive skin of her inner wrist and she felt her nipples tighten and tingle with awareness beneath her clothing. While he tried not to wince at the wall panels of pseudo-Georgian flowers picked out in lime-green and white, and the ludicrously opulent furniture which was so far removed from any Georgian ideal of elegance, Caroline was incapable of noticing anything.

Her face was flaming, shame and confusion having assailed her in a twin attack as her body reacted to the touch of his clever fingers. He had no idea of how inadequate she was and she dragged her hand free. Weighing up the potential future of the employees at Hales, however, Caroline ignored the twang of her conscience.

She had already warned Valente what she was like. It would be his own fault when he discovered that she was incapable of providing him with the level of sexual entertainment he expected. In any case he was trying to blackmail her, and she needed to use every possible weapon in her repertoire to fight back.

'I could never become your mistress,' she told him baldly. 'It would kill my parents. They're too old to handle that, Valente. Nor could they accept such a relationship and still live under this roof.'

Lean, strong face implacable, Valente moved back to the door. 'Why did you bring me in here?' His beautiful mouth took on a sardonic curl as he cast a speaking glance over the dusty reproduction sleigh bed, brilliant black eyes flicking up again to rest on her earnest face. He was unimpressed, for she had seemed equally sincere five years earlier when she told him how much she loved him. 'For a crazy moment I saw the bed and thought that maybe you wanted to pay me something on account…a first instalment, as it were.'

Consternation gripping her as he reached for the doorknob, Caroline blocked his passage while a blaze of temper roared through her. There it was again, the suggestion that she was a cheap and easy slut, and she hated him for it when she had given him no grounds to view her in that light. 'Why won't you talk to me or listen?' she hissed. 'I will do just about anything to protect the workers at Hales, but don't ask me to hurt or upset my parents. They could only accept the set-up you suggested if we got married!'

Valente flung back his arrogant dark head and laughed as though she had said something uproariously funny. '*Che idea!* I'm not the romantic I was five years ago, when you appealed to my protective instincts. Nor am I so hot for your tiny body that I would surrender my freedom for even a short period of time.'

Mortified colour flooded her cheeks when she appreciated that he had taken her declaration as a serious suggestion—which it had not been. It had simply occurred to her that the only way her parents would accept her intimacy with Valente or his financial help would be if he was her husband. In actuality the prospect of being married again, ensnared in a nightmare pretence of a relationship whilst being subjected to male demands, had as much attraction for Caroline as a dose of the plague, and she went white. She had hated being married, had felt trapped and helpless. But she found herself thinking that marrying Valente would be a much safer solution for her family than her becoming a mistress who might well be discarded within days, along with his generous promises. After all, she knew, even if he didn't, that she was the last woman alive likely to fulfil his fantasies in the bedroom.

'But then it wouldn't have to be a normal marriage... I mean one that lasts,' Caroline could not resist pointing out in a grudging undertone.

His sleek ebony brows pleated. '*Maledizione!* How could you seriously think that I would marry you?' he demanded with incredulous bite. 'Naturally I can understand why you would prefer that option. The divorce settlement would be worth millions, and we both know that although you hide it well there's nothing you wouldn't do for that amount of money!'

Barley able to credit that she was having such a conversion with Valente, Caroline fixed affronted grey eyes on him. 'I thought pre-nuptial agreements dealt with that sort of threat these days. I know you don't believe it, but I don't want your wretched money—'

'There's no way I would stoop to the level of

marrying you!' Valente spelt out with disdainful emphasis. 'You're a lying, deceitful, mercenary little witch. Get the idea of marriage right out of your head now.'

Caroline kept her head high. 'I'm afraid it's the only option I could accept—'

'But what would I get out of it—apart from a sense of self-sacrifice?' he fielded with unconcealed scorn, outraged by her cheek in even suggesting the idea, when she had stood him up at the altar five years earlier.

'Then accept that I will never be your mistress, Valente. Evidently we've reached stalemate.' Tilting her chin, Caroline opened the door and walked back out on to the landing with as much dignity as she could muster.

'I would want a child.'

Lashes flipping up in bewilderment over her startled eyes, Caroline froze in her tracks. She was stunned by that entirely unexpected announcement.

'An heir to follow in my phenomenally successful footsteps, *piccola mia,*' Valente mused silkily. 'How does that idea grab you?'

Caroline had turned pale, knowing that he had just presented her with yet another impossible challenge. 'It doesn't.'

Valente released a cruelly amused laugh. 'I didn't think it would, but that's the final offer on the table, *cara mia*. If I take you as a wife there has to be something more in it for me than sex. In that department I have endless choice and no reason to choose marriage. But a child would be the perfect sweetener to the deal.'

'Sadly, I'm not a whore or a brood mare.'

Valente cast her a lingering glance in the entrance hall. 'All women are capable of playing the whore for the right man…or the right opportunity. I wanted you the first time I saw you and I still want you. You've upped the stakes and so must I. I'll consider your idea if you spend the night with me at my hotel.'

Paralysed to the spot by that stunning proposition, Caroline gazed back at him with huge disbelieving eyes.

'I always play hardball, and if you want a wedding ring for what you can get out of me as a legally wedded gold-digger, I expect to preview the merchandise,' Valente delivered silkily. 'I'm tied up in meetings until ten tonight. I'll see you then.'

White as milk at that crack about merchandise, not to mention his belief that she had only mentioned marriage in the hope of reaping a greater financial profit from him, Caroline muttered, 'I couldn't possibly.'

'Final word, last chance,' he quipped, closing his arms round her slight body without warning and sealing her to his lean, powerful frame. 'The game is over, *angelina mia*. Take your chance while you can, because it won't come round again.'

Even a hint of what he probably saw as passion but she saw as potential coercion caused all the colour to bleed out of her complexion. It took every ounce of her self-command not to succumb to the urge to fight him off like an attacker. His strength, his very forcefulness, intimidated her. He dipped his mouth with comparative lightness down on to parted lips, and this time around she did not respond. In a sick daze of enforced tolerance, she was as still and unresponsive as a doll. Releasing his hold on her, he lifted his handsome dark head again, his shrewd, dark-as-night eyes arrowing over the frozen pallor of her face.

'Is this little demonstration your final answer?' Valente demanded, his musical, lilting Italian accent roughened and brusque in tone.

And she almost said yes. But something un-recognisable inside her surged up at the last moment with another answer entirely. It was an answer that took her aback almost as much as it surprised him. 'No…no, it's not!'

The fierce tension in Valente's tall, powerful physique eased infinitesimally. He turned to smoothly greet the men descending the stairs. A few minutes later the cars outside were pulling away and heading back down the drive. But Caroline was welded to the spot long after they had vanished from view. Her sense of horror at the invitation he had made in the most demeaning of terms had momentarily deprived her of the ability to think straight. And then the phone rang.

It was her parents. They had been invited to dine with her father's brother, Charles, who lived near the hospital, and would not be coming home until the following day. Her primary reaction was relief, and that shocked her, but she had no desire to discuss her meeting with Valente, or his visit to the house, as she knew she would have to lie about what had passed between them.

Only slowly did it dawn on her that she was now free to go to Valente's hotel—but of course she wouldn't do that. How could she? But Caroline's subconscious mind had long nour-

ished the disloyal suspicion that had she married
Valente rather than Matt her marriage would
have been consummated. It had been foolish to
believe that she and Matt could change overnight from platonic friends into keen bed
partners. Others more experienced with sex than
she had been might have managed that jump,
but she had failed miserably. From the first she
had been shy, awkward and inhibited, discovering too late that the physical response Valente
had awakened with ease had been sadly absent
with the man she married. Everything that could
go wrong had gone wrong between her and
Matt, and once that pattern had been set it had
been too late to change it.

What if it was different with Valente? Could
she be like any other woman with him? It was
an exciting question for a woman who was too
afraid to even consider dating, and had long
since assumed that she would be alone for the
rest of her life. She shrugged off the memory of
her moment of panic when Valente had last
kissed her, because she badly wanted to believe
that he could be the magic key to banish her inadequacy. What if she had a few drinks to loosen
up first? Wouldn't that give her more nerve and
take care of her shyness and inhibitions? All

she needed to do was get past that awful instant when panic threatened to sink in…

Bolstered by an inordinate amount of vodka, Caroline rebelled against the conservative wardrobe which Matt had insisted she should wear. He had made her feel old before her time, deeming make-up, nail varnish, shorter skirts and figure-flattering garments unsuitable for a married woman of her age. She reached into the back of the wardrobe for a dress she had bought when she was dating Valente, but which she had neither worn nor discarded. It was silvery blue, short, and it enhanced her slight curves. She left her hair down, the way she knew he liked it. Sheer tights and high-heeled sandals completed the look, but she was so startled when she saw her provocative reflection in the mirror she froze.

What sort of a woman dressed up for a one-night stand with a man who was planning to try her out as he might test-drive a new car? A really desperate woman, she acknowledged with a shame-faced shiver. It shook her that she might be even more desperate to discover whether she could be as sexy and desirable as any other woman than she was to become Valente's wife in order to help the Hales employees and her parents. What did *that* say about her?

A long, long time ago, before other influences prevailed, Valente had briefly transformed her into the woman she very much wanted to be. A strong woman, sure of her own judgement, ready to take the risk of loving and marrying a man who inhabited a totally different world from her own.

Her parents had gone off the deep end when they'd discovered she was dating one of the drivers at Hales. They had despised Valente even before they'd met him, making wild accusations against him and forming even wilder assumptions, saying he would only use and abuse her, insisting that he was only interested in marrying her because she stood to inherit Hales. A good part of their melodramatic reaction had been based on Valente's deprived background and lack of money, and Caroline had almost come to hate her parents for their arrogant prejudice.

Within weeks she had gone from being a devoted daughter to a deeply unhappy rebel, defying their demand that she give up Valente. But Matt had proved equally opposed to the relationship, and as he'd been a close friend his opinion had naturally influenced her.

'You don't have anything in common with him. He's not one of us,' Matt had argued loftily. 'You've never gone without anything you wanted. How could you possibly cope with the life you would have with him? And don't you owe your parents more than this? It's not unreasonable for them to want their only child to stay in the UK and marry an Englishman, willing to treat them with the respect and consideration they deserve!'

Gnawing guilt had taken the edge off her every moment with Valente, and then her feelings had swung violently against her parents when Hales had stopped giving work to Valente. She'd had no doubt that he was being deliberately excluded. He'd had to find other loads and runs to continue making a living and coming to the UK. That had been when she'd agreed to be his wife, outraged by the unjust treatment he had suffered at her family's hands.

Tearing herself free of those disturbing memories, and shrinking from an awareness of her immaturity and over-reliance on the opinions of others, Caroline studied her reflection in the mirror afresh and took another slug of vodka for good measure. She could be strong again. She could change everything around if she could just manage to share a bed with Valente for one night. Could that be so difficult? Once she had been madly in love with Valente. He was gorgeous. And surely he was so sexually experienced that he would soothe her nerves and help her to relax with him?

Downstairs the doorbell buzzed and she checked her watch. It was the taxi she had ordered. She descended the stairs, still feeling horribly sober and nervous, and wondered in dismay when the kick of the alcohol would hit and hopefully give her the backbone she lacked…

CHAPTER FOUR

WHILE a business report was being summarised for his benefit by a member of his personal team Valente checked his watch, his dark, reflective gaze continually straying to the entrance door to his hotel suite. The growing pressure at his groin increased in concert. Would Caroline dare to put in an appearance?

His wide, sensual mouth hardened into a sardonic line. He had set her a trap and he was keen to see if she would fall into it and drown. After all, if she was willing to respond to so demeaning a sexual summons, it pretty much proved that there was nothing she would not do to get her hands on his wealth. And if there was one field in which Valente Lorenzatto excelled, it was in his ability to spot women so greedy that they would mortgage their souls to the devil for money.

Caroline, however, existed on an altogether

more devious plane, and Valente had discovered that fact too late. Five years earlier he'd had complete faith in her. Indeed, her apparent vulnerability and innocence had charmed him, and that awareness still rankled. Right up until that day in the church it had never occurred to Valente that she might be a clever, deceitful fake—the kind of woman who would calculatingly pit one man against another to achieve her own ends. And the exercise had worked very well for her. Bailey, who'd had a womanising reputation, had got jealous and soon afterwards decided to marry her. Valente had learned the truth about Caroline the hard way, and this time around he was determined not to be influenced by crocodile tears or sad tales about her devoted parents.

Caroline got giggly in the hotel lift, and when she closed her eyes the world around her seemed to revolve. She so rarely touched alcohol—and never in quantity—that she was unsure whether she was mildly tipsy or guilty of having seriously overdone it. In addition, instead of discovering a new strain of confidence and sparkling sexiness, she felt nervous, abstracted and dizzy.

The door of the suite was opened not by

Valente, as she had expected, but by one of his staff. She walked with care in the high heels she wore. Valente's veiled dark eyes locked on to her, taking in the unbound tumble of her silvery blonde hair, lingering on the raspberry-tinted pout of her full mouth before skimming down to the swell of her breasts framed by the low neckline and the long silky length of leg revealed by the short skirt.

She took Valente's breath away: she was all woman, in a way he had never seen her before. Gone was the girlie-girl with the demure look he remembered, and gone was the stressed-out frumpy widow he had met that morning. From her shiny fall of pale hair to her huge misty grey eyes and the perfectly packaged little body below, she looked spectacular. The pressure at his groin became an aggressive throb of arousal. She had virtually nosedived into the trap he had set. He had not bargained on the discovery that he might fall into the same trap with her…for the desire to send her back home was nowhere to be found.

As she settled herself with surprising clumsiness into an armchair across the room, and her dress slid up over her slender thighs to expose more of their perfection than he wanted to share with his companions, Valente quickly dismissed his staff.

'Valente,' she whispered as the door closed on their departure. On her inviting lips the syllables of his name ran together with the suggestion of a slur. In his grey striped shirt—he had discarded both jacket and tie—he had a vital male presence that made her heart race. A five o'clock shadow of dark stubble roughened his handsome jawline and his tousled black hair was beginning to form curls. Through the fine cotton shirt she could see more than a hint of the dark whorls of hair outlining his powerful pectoral muscles. Matthew had liked to wax, but Caroline had always liked a man to look like a man, and few met the demands of that role as easily as Valente did. His height, breadth and strength, not to mention his strikingly handsome features, gave him a uniquely masculine quality of raw potent sexiness. Her mouth ran dry.

'I thought you wouldn't come,' he admitted with cruel candour.

Colour lining her cheekbones as she registered that he had been working, because he had really not expected her to meet his challenge, Caroline closed her hands together tightly. 'Obviously you're better at blackmail than you realise.'

'But one always has a choice, *cara mia,*' he reminded her lazily, watching her fingers dig into the back of her other hand and knowing she was drawing blood.

'Perhaps I should have told you to go to hell,' Caroline slung back, surprise at his attitude awakening her temper as well as a savaging sense of stupidity—because it seemed to her that he had only invited her as an exercise in humiliation.

'But you didn't,' Valente drawled, noting that she was slurring her words again and wondering if it was possible that she could have been drinking heavily. When he had known her she had hardly touched alcohol.

'It's not too late! Is this some sort of a game you play? You tell me what you want and once it's there you don't want it any more?' Caroline demanded shakily, because her brain was almost too befuddled to find the right words with which to fight her own corner.

Valente dealt her a wondering appraisal. 'Haven't you learned yet that that's what men are like?' he breathed. 'Most of us find that what we can't have is much more desirable.'

'I think I should leave.' Caroline reared upright in one driven movement, and in the same instant her stomach gave a violent lurch of nauseous response that made her skin break out in perspiration.

'*Porca miseria*...no!' Torn between by an attack of rampant indecision alien to him and a fierce desire to sate his sexual hunger without further ado, Valente sprang upright as well. He straightened just in time to see her sway. Her clear complexion had turned the colour of putty. 'What's wrong? Are you ill?'

'Bathroom...' she muttered urgently from behind the hand she had clamped betrayingly to her mouth.

Moments later Caroline fell awkwardly to her knees on the tiles that floored the pale designer bathroom and was horribly sick—sicker than she had ever been in her life. She was appalled by the exhibition she was making of herself, and in between the retches gasped horror-stricken apologies.

'Drunkenness is a big turn-off for me,' Valente declared icily from the doorway. 'Shout if you need assistance. Otherwise I'll wait in the drawing room.'

'Don't you have any compassion?' Big fat tears rolled down Caroline's face as she choked and spluttered in the misery of disgrace.

'No, and you would do well to remember the

fact,' he fielded without remorse, and the door snapped shut.

She had to hang onto the vanity unit to stay upright while she washed and freshened up as best she could. Although she had been sick, she still felt extremely unsteady on her feet. She took off her shoes and carried them.

Having resolutely banished the image of her suffering from his mind, Valente had returned to work on his laptop. He was in a very bad mood. The son of a father who had been an alcoholic, and abstemious in his own habits, he was disgusted by the state she was in. How *dared* she show up in that condition? How could she believe that such behaviour was acceptable to him? Did she think that he would want her at any cost, in any state, even drunk? For a male as fastidious as he was with women, it was an offence of no mean order.

She came into the room quietly, but he could still see how much of an effort it was for her just to put one foot in front of the other. His lean, breathtakingly handsome face hard as granite, he surveyed her with derision.

With half of her make-up washed off she was wan, and her smile was long gone. Barefoot, she no longer looked anything like a woman in her mid-twenties. She was so tiny, so delicate in build, with a ridiculously small waist and the fine bones of a bird. He shut off that dangerous train of sympathy-grabbing appreciation and flattened his expressive mouth into a stern line. This was the woman he would have married—the woman who probably would have been the mother of his first child by now.

'I'm sorry. I was foolish… I don't drink very often and I just drank far too much before I came out,' Caroline confided in a sudden desperate rush. 'I thought it would stop me being so nervous. I thought it would make me stronger—'

'You're not a teenager any more. You ought to know better,' Valente retorted drily. 'Drunks are never as entertaining as they imagine they are. You can't even walk in a straight line. It's not at all attractive.'

At that candid reminder, and still painfully aware of his merciless scrutiny, Caroline folded down on to the sofa beside her. She felt stiff and achy, and her head felt far too heavy for her neck. But more than anything she resented his attitude. After all, over the past forty-eight hours he had single-handedly put her through hell.

She lifted her chin, misty grey eyes bright

with condemnation. 'That's a shame, when it's your fault I got drunk in the first place.'

'How could it be my fault?' Valente growled, standing over her to stare down at her with judgemental dark eyes.

Caroline forgot her dizziness and leapt up again, clutching at the sofa-arm to steady her swaying legs. It was very much a case of mind over matter. 'You did this to me by threatening harm to everyone I care about and landing the responsibility for what happens to them on to my shoulders!'

'And such puny shoulders they are. Who would want to depend on *you*? I did once, and where did it get me?' Valente murmured lethally. 'You can't blame me for your weakness.'

Caroline was bone-white at having that particular flaw flung back in her face. 'When did you turn into such a total bastard? You don't care about anything or anybody as long as you get what you want.'

'The chances of my getting what I want at this moment look exceedingly remote,' Valente derided, averting his attention from the voluptuous appeal of her generous mouth and the lush swell of her round breasts. He cursed his powerful libido, and a body which had no conscience and no concept of self-protection, for he was already fiercely aroused. He crossed to the other side of the room to take up a position safely out of temptation's way. 'As far as I'm concerned, your state of intoxication makes you untouchable. Other men might be less choosy, but I'm not one of them.'

'Nothing I've done equals what you've done,' Caroline accused, holding herself rigid by the sofa in an effort to reclaim some dignity. It took even greater endeavour to think and vocalise, for her head was light and she felt as if the room was spinning round her again. Scarily, it was beginning to dawn on her that the full effects of the alcohol she had imbibed might not yet have hit her. 'You hate me. Why won't you let me explain what happened five years ago?'

'It's irrelevant after this length of time.'

'But I never got the chance to speak to you again because you'd returned to Italy. You even changed your mobile phone number. I wrote to you, though… I poured my heart out on paper. You never replied to my letters,' she reminded him painfully, thinking of the long weeks she had waited, praying for a reply, and the terrible silence that had underlined the fact that he was gone for ever.

'I chucked them in the bin unread. There was no point reading them. Some errors of judgement cannot be explained away or forgiven,' Valente pronounced with disdain, utilising a little white lie to conserve his privacy and to avoid having to deliberate over one very minor inexplicable aspect of his own behaviour.

'You really do hate me, don't you?' she pressed, huge pale silvery eyes focussed on him with disturbing intensity.

'I wouldn't waste that much emotion on you, *piccola mia*. What was done was done five years ago. Now, I think it's time for me to call my driver so that he can take you safely home,' Valente delivered.

'How can I go home when I don't know what's going to happen next?' Caroline exclaimed.

Valente dealt her an incredulous appraisal. 'If this was a trial view of what you might be like as a wife, you've bombed with spectacular effect.'

'I wouldn't want to marry you anyway!' Caroline yelled at him, full volume. 'I promised myself that I would never get married again because being tied to the wrong person is my definition of hell! Not to mention the fact that you're sarcastic, cold and callous, manipulative, hypocritical, unscrupulous and sexually deviant!'

'Sexually deviant?' Valente launched back at her, only troubling to argue that one phrase of her outraged description of his character.

'How else would a normal man describe summoning his former fiancée to a hotel like she's a prostitute?'

'Define "normal",' Valente invited. 'I'd say I'm still in that class, but possibly a little more adventurous and imaginative than most. If you hadn't wrecked it, it could have been a very sexy scenario.'

'For someone with no morals!' Caroline raged, finally into her stride and ignoring the horribly light-headed swirl she was in, and the fact that her view of Valente appeared to be coming and going and fogging over while her own voice had developed a horrible echo in her ears. 'I don't know how to do "very sexy", or "deviant", which is why I had to get drunk to come here. But I did it with the right intentions—to help other people.'

Valente was intrigued rather than repulsed by that feisty attack. He was also surprised to discover that the thought of teaching her how to do sexy and deviant in the bedroom had a tremendous appeal that had nothing at all to do with revenge, punishment or good business.

'To help other people?' he traded sardonically, unimpressed. 'Why do you always play the victim? You came here tonight because you were set on saving your own little carcass from the threat of homelessness and poverty, because you would very much enjoy the status and luxury of being my wife, and because, much as you want to deny it with your martyr act, you want a good excuse to get into my bed.'

'That's absolutely a lie!' Caroline snapped shrilly, taking a jerky, uncertain step forward—before crumpling down in a heap on to the carpet like a wind-up doll whose battery had suddenly gone flat.

For an instant Valente thought she was staging a bogus faint, like in the final shot of a melodrama, and he groaned out loud. But something about the stillness of her small shape drew him closer to examine her. He crouched down beside her inanimate body and tried to rouse her again. She had not tripped or struck her head, But when she failed to show any sign of life other than continuing to breathe, grudging concern coloured his cynicism. He rang Reception and asked for a doctor to be called. Offered first aid assistance, he gave a negative answer. If, as he suspected, alcohol was the cause of her collapse, the fewer people who knew about it the better. He picked her up, only to be troubled by how little her slight body weighed, and carried her into the bedroom. He studied her stillness, wondering if he should have called an ambulance instead, or even if he should just be bundling her into his limo to head to the local A&E himself.

The smudged mascara couldn't hide the purple shadows below her eyes that accentuated her pallor, or the reality that, with the exception of breast and hip, she was exceedingly thin. It was barely five minutes before a doctor arrived at the door; by chance, the older man had been checking in at Reception when Valente had called down and, having overheard the conversation, had offered his services.

Dr Seaborne took one frowning look at his diminutive patient and asked what age she was. Valente was outraged at having to rifle through Caroline's bag to provide proof of her age on her driving licence before the man was satisfied that he was not some predator with a preference for underage girls. In the midst of that interrogation her mobile phone began ringing. Valente switched it off.

Deeply unimpressed by his inebriated patient, the doctor checked Caroline over as best as he could, and said that he saw no point seeking further medical help simply because she had passed out.

Although severely ruffled by the treatment he had received for the sin of harbouring a very youthful-looking drunk in his hotel suite, Valente knew he could not possibly have her delivered home unconscious without being forced to make the sort of explanation he had no intention of making to her parents. Furious with her for landing him into such an untenable situation, he stripped off her dress and slotted her into the bed—but not before wincing at her unexciting white underwear topped by the sin of tights rather than the tantalising appeal of stockings…

Caroline had to break through layers of discomfort to battle into full wakefulness. Her head ached, her mouth was dry as a bone and her stomach felt distinctly sensitive. Pulling herself up against the pillows with a moan of self-pity, she opened her eyes on a totally unfamiliar room. In a panic, she lurched out of bed, blinking in dismay as her head swam just a little—and she recoiled in horror when the bedroom door opened wider to frame Valente.

'I heard you get up. I'll order breakfast for you.'

In the act of trying to wrap herself in the duvet in a hurry, her face hot enough to fry eggs on, Caroline reeled back against the bed for support. 'No, thanks,' she said weakly, appalled to acknowledge that she had failed to go home the night before and that she remembered next to nothing about their meeting after being ill.

Exotically, wildly handsome, and extremely well-groomed in his black designer-cut suit and cerise silk shirt, Valente leant back against the doorjamb like a model straight out of a glossy magazine. 'Eat. It'll make you feel better, and possibly a couple of painkillers would help too.'

'Why didn't you take me home?' Caroline gasped, looking anywhere but at him. And in the midst of that evasive activity she finally noticed that the pillow beside hers bore the imprint of a head. 'My goodness…no—we slept together?'

'The sofa was too small for me.'

Caroline settled aghast grey eyes on him. 'Did we…? I mean…?'

Valente gave her a slicing look of derision. 'Do I look so desperate for sex that I would make use of a comatose body?'

As he had no doubt intended, Caroline

shrank again, and hugged the duvet all the tighter to her shivering figure. 'So we didn't, then. That's good,' she managed to say.

'Quite.' A slanting ebony brow lifted. 'But don't ever drink like that again.'

'I won't,' she said tightly. 'It was a hideous mistake, and I learn from my mistakes.'

'Some men would have taken advantage of you in that condition. You were in no state to look after yourself and that's dangerous,' he framed harshly.

'Right…okay…message more than received,' Caroline countered, squirming with shame. 'If it's all right with you I'm going to take a shower.'

Valente waved a helpful hand in the right direction. 'Breakfast will be waiting when you're ready.'

After stooping to pick up the silver-blue dress from the floor, Caroline wore the duvet into the bathroom. Only then did she wonder what time it was, and take on board the reality that she had stayed out all night. Her watch let her know it was only eight o'clock, and she knew her parents were unlikely to get home until lunchtime at the earliest since her Uncle Charles was an elderly bachelor and a most gracious host. Thanking her lucky stars for that reality, Caroline shed the concealment of the duvet and stepped into the shower.

What a disaster she had been in the seduction stakes! How could she have been so foolish as to drink so much? If anything she had damaged her own cause irreparably, because now Valente was disgusted with her. So, once more, the virtue she no longer wanted had been conserved. A shiver of regret ran through her at the thought of how unattractive her behaviour must have been. It wasn't that she particularly *wanted* to be attractive to Valente, she reasoned doggedly, only that that supposed attraction appeared to be the only bargaining chip she had.

Putting on the previous night's clothes was not a pleasurable exercise either. She did the best she could with her hair, but the mirror warned her that too much alcohol had given her a pale, puffy face that looked both plain and tired. She reluctantly joined Valente in the dining annexe off the drawing room. He handed her painkillers and a glass of water first, and she took them without comment because she still felt awful. A large selection of food was on offer, and she nibbled modestly at a few items in the vague hope of settling her stomach.

While she ate, and he drank copious amounts of black coffee, Valente described the doctor's concerns of the evening before, and before very long she wanted once again to sink through the floor in shame.

'Your phone was ringing last night. I switched it off,' he told her finally.

Caroline hadn't even checked her phone, and she fished it out of her bag and switched it on again. She frowned when she realised she had missed a whole heap of calls. Cold, clammy anxiety gripped her when she realised that her Uncle Charles and on two occasions her mother had made those calls, in an unsuccessful but clearly urgent attempt to get in touch with her.

'What is it?' Valente prompted.

Caroline was already frantically clicking on her uncle's number.

The older man answered his phone quickly. 'Caroline? Thank goodness I've finally got hold of you,' he exclaimed, before telling her that her father had suffered what Charles referred to as 'a funny turn' the evening before, and had been taken into hospital. Her mother had accompanied her husband, and had already phoned Charles that morning to ask if he thought she ought to call the police because she couldn't get hold of her daughter.

'I'll go straight to the hospital,' Caroline stated, in a daze of disbelief and horror at what had been happening while she lay asleep.

'Hospital?' As she stood up, Valente closed a hand round her arm to still her. 'What's going on?'

Her eyes brimming with guilty tears of anxiety, Caroline explained in harried tones while dialling the number of the hospital which her uncle had given her. She wanted to ensure that her mother would receive a message of re-assurance as soon as possible.

'I'll take you there right now,' Valente declared, contacting his staff in turn to issue instructions. 'Why would your mother have wanted to call the police, though? Do you never stay out overnight?'

'Of course not. I didn't worry about last night because I assumed they were safe at Charles's house. I should have known better,' she lamented, her conscience eating her alive because she had not been available to offer help and support when she was needed. 'Now they'll know I didn't come home, and they'll be terribly shocked and upset by that. Who am I supposed to say I was with? If I admit it was you, it'll be like Armageddon.'

'You're an adult, not a child, *piccola mia*. An explanation shouldn't be necessary. You were married for several years.' Brilliant dark eyes assailed her and her tummy somersaulted in response. 'I can hardly believe that you are still allowing your parents to rule you to this extent.'

'It's not like that!' Caroline proclaimed angrily. 'I rarely go out at night, and they know I don't have a boyfriend, so of course they would worry when they discovered that I wasn't at home in the middle of the night. Unlike you, I lead a very quiet life. Why on earth did you switch off my phone?'

'The doctor I had summoned to attend to you was waiting to speak to me, and you were in no fit state to deal with a phone call.'

His argument was unanswerable.

Caroline hung her head. 'I feel so cheap, walking out of a hotel dressed in last night's clothes. Everybody will know I've had a one-night stand.'

'I should be so lucky,' Valente quipped, soft and low. 'The minute we got together it was guaranteed to go wrong. There could not be two more different people on this planet than you and I.'

In the grand foyer on the ground floor, Caroline tried to behave like the invisible woman for the benefit of any interested parties who might choose to regard her as a slut for being seen wearing a cocktail dress at breakfast time. Valente, however, closed a hand over hers and urged her into the hotel boutique.

'I called ahead,' he breathed as a saleswoman approached them with a smile.

'Mr Lorenzatto? I believe we have exactly what you're looking for.'

With a smile, she extended a dressy sapphire-blue raincoat for Caroline to try on.

Caroline was duly inserted into the coat and the sash pulled tight at her waist. 'Perfect,' Valente pronounced, flexing a gold credit card before urging her back into the foyer again.

'I'll have to pay you for this,' Caroline muttered uncomfortably, but she was relieved to have the means of concealing a dress that would have looked highly suspicious to her mother.

'You don't ever pay,' Valente riposted. 'That's the main advantage of being the mistress of a very rich man.'

'I didn't know I was still in the running,' Caroline said breathlessly, suddenly aware that his staff and security team were all waiting beside the fleet of cars parked at the front of the hotel, and eying her with intense curiosity. She blushed to the roots of her hair.

Valente noted that every man in their radius was unashamedly staring at the little figure by his side. Even when she made no effort to attract masculine attention she oozed femininity, cuteness and sex appeal from every pore. He clenched his even white teeth hard. Just minutes earlier he had been thinking that enough was enough, and he didn't want to be involved in the complexities of any form of relationship with Caroline. But the thought of leaving her free, if poor, to be scooped up by some other man had zero attraction for him.

He turned smouldering dark golden eyes on her again. 'But you want to stay in the running, don't you?'

Her lashes swept up on her bright eyes and she nodded very slowly in agreement, although she couldn't quite believe what she was doing.

'So,' Valente breathed huskily, 'you believe that you can do better than last night?'

'Oh, yes,' Caroline told him blithely, refusing to give way to her usual sense of failure and low expectation.

His own expectations on a stimulating sexual

high, Valente smiled wolfishly down at her for the first time since that unforgotten solitary vigil at the church.

CHAPTER FIVE

'YOU don't need to come in with me,' Caroline told Valente as the limousine drew up outside the hospital.

Valente simply ignored the statement.

Almost running to keep up with his long stride, Caroline made a second attempt to deter him before they reached Reception. 'You must have loads of more important things to do,' she said breathlessly.

Valente discovered on which ward her father was from a receptionist, who gave him the kind of star-struck treatment a famous celebrity might have received for an unannounced visit. At a trot, to match his ground-breaking progress through the busy corridors, Caroline clutched at his jacket-sleeve to bring him to a halt. 'You can't let Mum and Dad see you. You can't let them know I was with you last night.'

He gave her anxious face a long, steady scrutiny. 'Are you a child or an adult?'

'This is not about me or you—it's about my father's health. He mustn't have any shocks or upsets right now. He's on a waiting list for heart surgery,' she explained in an urgent undertone.

'I would still like to speak to your parents...'

'You're the guy who owns their business and is about to chuck them out of their home,' she reminded him bluntly. 'Why would they want to see you when they're already worried sick about Dad's health?'

Finally, Valente agreed to wait round the corner from the side ward where she was directed to find her father. From there, however, once the curtains round the bed were partially drawn back, he had a perfect view of Joe Hales. The older man's face was an unhealthy colour, his rasping breathing audible even from where Valente stood. Joe was wired up to a monitor; his wife was seated by his side. Valente was shocked by how much Caroline's parents had aged since he had last seen them. Isabel had shrunk in stature even more.

But as Caroline's mother broke into urgent speech, Valente soon appreciated that she might have become thinner, and her back more bent with her advancing years, but her abrasive controlling personality had not mellowed at all.

'Where were you last night?' Isabel demanded accusingly. 'We've been worried sick about you.'

'Now, now…' Joe Hales interposed, striving to give his daughter a reassuring smile from blue-tinged lips as Caroline squeezed his hand affectionately. 'We don't want her sitting home every night at her age.'

'I had a meeting with Valente,' Caroline responded, striving to stick to the truth as far as she could. 'I knew you were staying with Uncle Charles and I switched my phone off. I'm so sorry you weren't able to get in touch with me.'

'You went behind our backs to see that Italian?' her mother hissed, in a tone of furious disbelief.

'But you knew that I was seeing Valente yesterday morning,' Caroline pointed out in a quiet, defensive tone, aimed at reminding Isabel that raised voices could be clearly heard through the rest of the ward. 'How are you feeling, Dad?'

'Tired, that's all. Your mother's been a tower of strength,' Joe declared, endeavouring to calm his wife down with a change of topic.

'We can't just let this go. It's a matter of decency,' Isabel pronounced truculently. 'I refuse to have any conversation with you at all,

Caro, until you tell us why you didn't come home last night.'

A pulsing silence fell while Caroline attempted to come up with a convincing story. Could she pretend that she had been at Winterwood all along and simply hadn't heard the phone ringing? Shouldn't she be adult enough to stand her ground and insist on her right to some privacy? It was not the time or the place. The look in her mother's cold blue eyes cut like glass through Caroline's frantic guilty thoughts, panicking her, making her feel like the worst daughter in the world, while once again making her painfully aware that she would never know happiness until she had garnered the strength to stand her ground against such domination. The ensuing awful silence, which she did not know how to fill, cut at her nerves like a slashing whip.

Valente brushed back the curtains and took up position by her side, greeting her parents with a cool and calm that knocked Caroline sideways before saying, 'Last night I wouldn't let Caroline go back to an empty house. Winterwood is remote, with your nearest neighbour living a considerable distance away. In your absence, I thought it made more sense for Caroline to spend the night at the hotel.'

Her eyes fiery, Isabel Hales opened her mouth to speak and closed it again only when her husband leapt thankfully on that explanation, which fitted in beautifully with his old-fashioned outlook. He found it perfectly acceptable that Valente should be protective towards his daughter. 'That was the best idea in the circumstances. No harm done,' Joe pronounced with relief, his eyes sliding shut, as if he was struggling to stay awake, and then slowly opening again.

'Of course Caroline protested,' Valente quipped.

'Y-yes,' Caroline stammered, overpowered by his intervention and his ready wits. 'Dad, you look like you need to get some sleep.'

'Let me offer you a lift home.' Valente addressed Isabel Hales. 'You must be exhausted if you've been here all night.'

'Joe needs me,' Isabel delivered, with a suspicious look at the tall, broad Italian.

'I'll be all right. You should come back later,' her husband urged, reaching out a hand to grasp his wife's in a reassuring gesture.

Valente noted the glitter of tears in Isabel's gaze

and registered that she had a human side after all.
For all her seeming superficiality and affectation,
she was deeply attached to her husband.

Isabel was stiff and sore after sitting for so
long, and required her daughter's support to
stand up and walk with her stick. She spoke to
the ward sister on the way out, and they left the
hospital at a much slower pace than when they
had arrived. Caroline was amazed that her
mother had agreed to accept a lift home from
Valente, but, spotting the tremulous line of the
older woman's mouth, recognised that her
energy resources were dwindling.

Once Isabel Hales became aware that
Valente's preferred mode of travel was a limousine, with accompanying security staff, she was
much more forthcoming and chatty. Caroline
was astonished when her mother broke into
animated conversation and smiled, as if Valente
was an old friend rather than someone she had
only recently professed to despise. It soon
dawned on her that her mother was hopelessly
impressed by Valente's evident wealth and she
was mortified, painfully conscious that Valente
was quite capable of making the same shameful
and embarrassing deduction.

Having insisted on assisting her mother from

the car and walking her to the front door, Valente rested a lean, possessive hand on Caroline's slight shoulder and bent down to say, 'I'll phone you tomorrow.'

Looking up to find black-lashed dark golden eyes intent on her, Caroline trembled and felt the pound of her heartbeat behind her breastbone. All of a sudden it was a challenge to speak or breathe, and instinct made her pull away as if he was crowding her—which indeed he was. 'There's no need.'

'There's every need,' Valente contradicted, without a second of hesitation.

'I'll be at the hospital with Dad.'

'But you will hardly be there all day,' Isabel Hales interposed in a tone of admonishment.

'I have an order of jewellery to finish before Friday,' Caroline added tautly, incredulous at her mother's sudden alarming change in attitude.

'We'll have dinner together tomorrow evening, *bella mia*. I'll send the car to pick you up at seven,' Valente countered.

'Mum, what are you doing?' Caroline pressed in a driven undertone the instant the front door had flipped shut behind the two women.

'What are *you* doing?' Isabel enquired in

dulcet return. 'Your one-time lorry driver is now filthy rich and just as keen as he ever was…'

'Of course he isn't!' Caroline snapped, bending down to pet Koko, who had come bounding up gracefully to greet her return.

The older woman gave her an amused glance. 'This is not the time to be shy, Caro. I saw how he looks at you. He owns our business. He owns our home. You're working your fingers to the bone with that wretched jewellery enterprise and you're as poor as a church mouse. A rich husband would solve all our problems very nicely.'

'No—no, he wouldn't!' Caroline repudiated that audacious suggestion with rare vehemence, causing her mother to raise a minatory brow. 'I've got no intention of ever marrying again!'

'Not all men are like Matthew,' Isabel said drily as Caroline was heading for the stairs.

With Koko cradled in her arms and purring like a steam engine, Caroline stilled and slowly turned round. 'What do you mean by that?'

In the act of walking into the sitting room, Isabel heaved a sigh. 'Naturally I knew that Matthew had other…shall we say…interests? The PA with the large chest whom he hired at such great expense? The blowsy barmaid down at The Swan? The garage-owner's wife? Need I continue?'

'No. I had no idea you knew. You never said anything.' The delicate bones of Caroline's face had set hard, and a sense of deep humiliation was creeping over her. Her mother's calmness as she took a seat amazed her daughter almost as much as the extent of her knowledge about her late son-in-law's extra-marital affairs. As her grip on the elegant Siamese cat tightened, Koko made a little cry of complaint and leapt down to the carpet to stalk angrily away, tail held rigidly upright to express her disapproval.

'It was none of my business—' Isabel contended.

Something sharp pierced Caroline and freed up her temper. 'Wasn't it?' she interrupted, with a bitterness that she usually kept hidden. 'You raved about Matthew. You thought he was perfect because he had a private education and a well-bred accent. You never looked beyond the surface. You persuaded me that my friendship with Matthew would make a much batter basis for marriage than what you called my "wild infatuation" with Valente!'

As Caroline's voice rose in volume, Isabel

frowned. 'Control yourself, Caro. I'm willing to admit that Matthew was something of a disappointment as a son-in-law, but you could hardly expect me to have guessed that he had a secret fetish for sluttish women with big bosoms!'

White as a sheet at that unexpectedly blunt reminder of her late husband's preferences, Caroline quivered with the fierceness of the emotions she was fighting to suppress. 'Why didn't you tell me that you knew? It would have made such a difference to me if I'd been able to confide in you.'

'I wouldn't have wanted to discuss something so distasteful. You already knew what to do. Like a sensible wife, you turned a blind eye. It was nothing to do with me.' For the second time, Isabel denied any responsibility.

Caroline spun away, her eyes burning. She had not initially chosen to turn a blind eye. Matthew had refused to tolerate what he'd angrily labelled as 'interference' in his private life. Time and time again her husband had reminded her that she was an abnormal wife, and that *she* had driven him into seeking out other women who could give him what he needed. And the women Matthew had found truly attractive had been the very opposite of

Caroline—outgoing, sexually skilled and voluptuous women, willing to try everything that Caroline was not. Just thinking about how trapped she had felt with him, once he was running her family's business and seemingly the very apple of their eyes, made Caroline feel nauseous.

'You and Matthew had so much in common. It should've been a match made in heaven. His parents certainly thought so,' Isabel remarked with regret. 'And we thought Matthew would be perfect for our needs as well.'

Caroline's brow pleated. 'Your needs?' she queried.

'Don't be naïve, Caro,' Isabel censured. 'Naturally we always hoped you'd bring home a husband who could take over the firm for us. Matthew was from the right background and he had great management experience.'

Caroline was studying the older woman in growing horror. 'Is that why you were so keen on me marrying him?'

'You were very attached to him. You'd known him all your life.'

'Why did Matthew's parents suddenly decide to invest in Hales when we got married?' Caroline cut in tightly.

'They wanted him to settle down, and we were all keen for him to take over the business. It was a natural development.'

'Was it really?' her daughter replied, less than convinced, belatedly conscious that her marriage had included an 'understanding' and a business angle between the two families that she had remained utterly unaware of at the time.

'Giles Sweetman was already nearing retirement when he left us, and your father thought the firm was ready for a shake-up. Matthew was young and dynamic.'

'So the Baileys only invested in the firm because Matthew was taking over as manager. Is that the only reason he wanted to marry me?'

An angry flush marked the older woman's cheeks. 'Don't be ridiculous, Caro. Matthew loved you—'

'No,' Caroline cut in flatly. 'He never loved me. I can assure you of that. But he had expensive tastes, and his parents were getting tired of keeping him. I can see that back then it would've seemed worth his while to marry me when I was coming to him with Hales as a dowry.'

'My goodness, what an imagination you have!' Isabel exclaimed. 'It wasn't like that at all.'

Caroline choked back the furious words

ready to leap on to her tongue and gritted her teeth, for she could see no point in arguing about a marriage that was no longer in existence. 'I'm going up to bed now.'

'I don't know what's the matter with you.'

'No, you've never understood me,' Caroline said painfully.

'Oh, don't go all pathetic,' Isabel sniped in exasperation. 'Your father and I thought we were doing the very best we could for you when we encouraged you to marry Matthew—you used to call him your best friend!'

'I loved Valente,' Caroline said shakily, a great frightening wave of emotion washing through her.

'And going by what I saw today you can still have him…if you're clever enough to reel him in again,' Isabel responded with superior amusement.

Caroline got into bed and cried for her own stupidity, while Koko made plaintive cries in sympathy. Caroline saw that five years earlier she had got caught like a fly in a spider's web. Both sets of parents had had a good reason for encouraging a marriage between their offspring. The Haleses had got a healthy investment sum to bolster their transport firm, in return for the assurance that Matthew would soon be in charge of it and its ultimate owner as their son-in-law. The Baileys had wanted a safe niche for Matthew, who had demonstrated a worrying in-ability to settle down to one job and stick to it, and of course they had also wanted a grand-child. Only Caroline had been too naïve to spot the reality that her marriage was much more a business agreement than a relationship between two people. It infuriated and shamed her that she had not had the wit to see that background at the time.

She spent a good deal of the following day with her father, waiting patiently while he underwent tests and soothing him in the after-math, for he hated being told to rest. Early af-ternoon she returned home to her workshop, to finish the order she had to complete. It was only when that was achieved that she allowed herself to recall that she was due to have dinner with Valente in less than an hour.

'Are you only bothering to get ready now?' Isabel snapped in disbelief when she saw her daughter heading upstairs. 'You look a total mess!'

'Thanks,' Caroline replied.

'Even beautiful girls have to make an effort,'

the older woman scolded. 'You haven't had your hair done, or your nails.'

Caroline gazed down stonily at her mother. 'The only thing you ever had against Valente was that he was poor. Now he's rich he's acceptable—more than acceptable.'

'If you intend to keep on harping back to the past, I've got nothing more to say to you. But you need to make more of an effort to hold on to a man, Caro,' Isabel spelt out sharply. 'Maybe Matthew would have stayed home more often if you had paid more attention to your grooming.'

Such words spoken by her mother, who must have known all along how unhappy her daughter was in her marriage, stung Caroline like a hard slap in the face. She continued up to her bedroom and rifled the wardrobe without much interest to find something to wear. There was nothing stylish. Matthew, so profligate in his own habits and tastes away from home, had insisted that his wife wore plain clothes in the style his mother wore: skirts and sweaters, stiff formal dresses. She yanked out a cream brocade long-sleeved dress and jacket she had once worn to a wedding and went for a shower.

Matthew, she recognised for the first time,

had been a bully, who had sapped her of energy and fight by continually undermining her. Her in-laws had blamed *her* for his constant absences, often suggesting that a child would have kept him home more. Caroline rather thought that a child would have made Matthew, who had been so determined not to grow up, run for the hills. Her marriage had been a blame game in which she'd been held responsible for everyone else's sins and disappointments. And she would never know whether Matthew would have remained faithful if she had not been frigid in bed. Frigid. Such an awful, inappropriate word, Caroline reflected while she dried her hair and straightened it. It didn't seem to her that that word came anywhere near describing the awful squirming panic and fear that consumed her at the threat of sex. She shivered, thinking again that it was so very typical of Valente to want what he could not have.

With a modicum of make-up applied, Caroline slid her feet into low-heeled cream shoes and went down to climb into the waiting limousine. Before she left her mother called her into the sitting room to say, 'I'll understand if you're very late, but if you'll take my advice you'll be very restrained in your behaviour.'

Caroline almost laughed out loud with a scorn that was new to her. Here was her manipulative mother, telling her with the utmost hypocrisy that it was all right to sleep with Valente but that she believed saying no would keep him more safely hooked. But now it was her father whom Caroline was most concerned about, as he had none of her mother's steel. If Hales shut down he would take it hard, because he would blame himself for the predicament of his former employees. What would that stress and sense of responsibility do to his heart? Caroline had to confront the risk that her father might die before he underwent the surgery that would prolong his life, and that awareness shook her up badly.

Valente watched Caroline cross the dining room to join him. Her outfit, a good deal less daring than the dress she had worn the night before, was fashioned of heavy brocade, covering her to wrist, throat and knee, and was as shapeless as a tube, barely hinting that there might be a female body beneath. Her hair, however, lay like a glossy cloud on her shoulders and framed her exquisite face. He met her huge grey eyes across the floor and recognised that she was as on edge as a condemned prisoner being herded to the gallows. It was an image that both disturbed and offended a man accustomed to female admiration and desire.

Caroline recognised the dark glow of appreciation in Valente's intent gaze. It intimidated her, unnerved her, only reminding her of her own inability to respond. She was all covered up, nothing on show, but her modest apparel had failed to snuff out his interest.

'That dress is so horrible I just want to rip it off you,' Valente confided while Caroline was attempting to peruse the menu handed to her.

Caroline paled and lifted eyes that were so frankly fearful to his lean, darkly handsome face that he was pushed into adding, 'That was a joke…okay? A joke with a sting, *piccola mia*. I look forward to seeing you dressed in designer clothes that fit you properly.'

'I've lost weight since Matthew died…hardly anything I have fits,' she confided, some of her tension easing at that explanation even while the frightening image of having her clothes ripped off struck her as ridiculous and finally faded from her mind.

He scored a lean forefinger over the back of her clenched hand, where it rested on the polished wood of the table. She trembled, feeling the tingling effect of his light touch the whole length of her arm. 'Try to relax. You're making me nervous.'

'I didn't think that was possible.'

'With you, anything is possible,' Valente riposted. 'Are you worried about your father?'

Caroline grimaced. 'Of course I am. He needs surgery urgently.'

'But he is being treated by a state hospital, where there is probably a waiting list for such operations, and he will need to build up his strength before he can have one,' Valente reminded her, for he had been present when her mother had spoken to the consultant the day before. 'I could pay for that surgery privately, and your father could have it as soon as he was ready.'

Sheer surprise made Caroline blink, before focusing intently on his bronzed features and the stunning golden eyes fixed to her. 'I can't believe you're offering me something like that—'

'Why not? Whatever it takes, I want you back in my life.'

Her smooth brow indented, for he was so far removed from her in his way of thinking that she was appalled. 'But you can't bargain with people's lives, Valente. Nobody should do that.'

Valente lounged back in his chair, black-lashed eyes reduced to a daunting sliver of hot gold resolve and challenge. 'Whatever it takes,' he repeated silkily, stubbornly unrepentant.

And that was the moment Caroline realised that he had made her an offer she could not in all conscience refuse…

CHAPTER SIX

'YOU'VE WON,' Caroline conceded in a driven admission. 'There's nothing I wouldn't do to keep my father alive.'

'That's admirable, *gioia mia.* I admire loyalty,' Valente countered smoothly. 'That only leaves the terms to be discussed.'

Caroline wanted to empty the water jug over him, because he made no attempt to hide his strong satisfaction. Winning meant a great deal to Valente Lorenzatto, and he scared her because his ruthlessness appeared to respect no boundaries. By 'terms', he meant mistress or wife. He was driving her in a direction she did not want to go. For her own safety, she needed an arrangement which could not be set aside in the space of a moment. A mistress was too easily discarded—and she was convinced that he *would* quickly want to discard her, cutting her out of his life as quickly as he had come back into hers.

Valente wanted and expected only pleasure from her sex. In the past, women had fawned over him for his dark, sexy good-looks and potent personality. Sixth sense had warned her even then that he had enjoyed many conquests. Now, with the addition of wealth and position, Valente had to be downright irresistible to her sex. After all, even *she* was not totally impervious to his magnetic attraction. Although coping with a few gentle kisses was a far different challenge from sharing a bed and the ultimate intimacy with him, she acknowledged apprehensively.

The first course was served. Held by the dark shrewd gleam of Valente's unyielding gaze, Caroline pushed the plate away.

'Eat,' he urged immediately, reaching across the table to push the plate back towards her again. 'You're as thin as a cardboard cut-out.'

Her face flamed. 'I'm naturally thin.'

'When I lifted you last night, you felt as light as a child in my arms.'

'Your concern is nonsensical. I'm quite happy with myself the way I am,' Caroline told him tartly, wondering if his tastes in women ran in the same direction as her late husband's. She shuddered at the recollection of Matthew's cruelly cutting comments about her boyish lack of curves.

'If you're planning to demand that I marry you, you'll need to be a healthy weight to conceive,' Valente pointed out coolly. 'But I hope that isn't the option you're thinking of choosing.'

'Why?' Caroline asked starkly.

Valente slotted a knife and fork into her empty hands with military precision and no lack of determination. 'I'm being honest. I don't want to marry you. I'm not the same person I was five years ago. I don't think the same. I don't feel the same, either.'

Hotly flushed in receipt of that blunt rejection, coming at her even before she had voiced her own feelings, Caroline breathed, 'You're telling me. You used to be much warmer and more caring.'

'Only those sterling qualities didn't get you to the church on time,' Valente fired back with sardonic bite, watching her eyes fall from his in discomfiture. He smiled a razor-edged smile. 'I don't want a wife. I want a mistress. I will be much more generous if you come to me on my terms.'

Caroline swallowed hard and skimmed her gaze round the dining room, noting that several women were looking in their direction, with Valente providing the focus for their attention. Other women would always want him, she reflected unhappily. And now she was about to work a confidence trick on him—because, while she might rail against his ruthlessness, wasn't it dishonest of her to opt for marriage when she knew that she was unlikely to consummate it? Shame filled her, closely backed by fear, for she dreaded entering the minefield of matrimony again and the threatening challenge of the marital bed.

Valente watched her, trying to read the significance of her lowered lashes and the quivering vulnerability of her very kissable ripe pink mouth. It had been a torture to lie beside her without touching her the previous night. He had only to imagine what he would do with her when he got the opportunity and his body hardened instantly, the fierce, urgent arousal that had already disturbed his sleep for two nights returning to dig talon claws of very real hunger into his tall, powerful frame. What was it about her that made her so much more sexually alluring than other women?

But marriage would be a ridiculously high price to pay for fulfilment, he conceded grimly.

In all likelihood the slaking of his desire for her would result in a rapid cooling-off of his interest, and a wife was not as easily shed as a mistress. On the other hand a child from such a marriage would ensure that he did not have to tie himself down on a more permanent basis to another woman in the future. It was imperative that he have a child at some stage to continue the family line, protect the extensive Barbieri estates for the next generation, and take charge of his own vast business empire.

'It would have to be marriage.' Caroline had to force out her final answer, because cheating didn't come naturally to her and she was convinced that what she was doing was just that. But he had offered to cover the cost of her father's heart surgery, to let her parents remain at Winterwood, and to ensure that jobs were safe at Hales Transport. It was his own fault that he had heaped the scales so heavily in his own favour. How could she possibly turn him down? He had the power to turn all their lives around, but if she married him he would also have the power to destroy her and complete the task that Matthew had begun.

In negotiation mode, Valente studied her like a cat studied a mouse getting ready to make a break for freedom. 'Why?'

Feeling too warm under such pressure, Caroline unbuttoned her jacket and slid out of it, revealing a tantalising amount of bare skin, for the dress beneath was not as modest in cut when she bent down to eat. 'Dad would never accept the other option. He's an old-fashioned man…'

'Plenty of couples live together these days without a wedding ring.' Valente feasted his eyes shamelessly on the stimulating view of the rounded globes of her breasts and imagined having the right to touch and stimulate that sweet soft flesh. If he married her she would always be available, not just waiting at the end of a phone line for his call. It was a seductive thought, and the pressure that built at his groin was an exquisite pain.

'I don't think I could trust you to keep your promises unless I was your wife,' Caroline stated forthrightly, and set down her knife and fork, amazed to discover that she had cleared her plate.

Valente was shocked out of his erotic reverie by that comeback.

Her grey eyes were silvery pale as frost and full of challenge, her fragile bone structure tautly outlined below her fair skin.

'You don't trust me,' he said, unamused.

'You don't trust me, either.'

'I won't be a great husband.'

'As long as you're not violent or abusive I can cope with that.'

Valente's black luxuriant lashes dropped down to conceal his startled gaze. For the first time he felt an acute stab of curiosity to know more about her marriage to Matthew Bailey. 'I will be neither.'

'We're agreed, then?' Caroline prompted anxiously.

There was a cool, unforgiving darkness in his measuring gaze. 'We'll get married as soon as it can be arranged.'

'Did you mean it when you said you wanted a child?' she whispered after the next course was served, for she was barely able to believe that he had agreed to her option.

'*Si, gioia mia*. There has to be some advantage for me in the arrangement.'

In the circumstances it was crazy, but she felt hurt by the cold calculation of that declaration. He talked and behaved as if he wanted her at any cost, but quite evidently his intelligence ruled him more than his passion if he could say such a thing. She was outraged by his assumption that providing him with a child could be styled as an acceptable demand in any agreement. Yet she saw no point in arguing, because she was convinced that he would soon cancel their agreement and divorce her when she disappointed him in the bedroom. They would never get near the stage of conceiving a child, which meant that once again she would be letting him down. It was a thought that cut through Caroline like a knife. All of a sudden it seemed to her that no matter what she did, she did it wrong.

At the end of the meal Valente insisted on taking her home, accompanying her out of the hotel with a light hand at her spine and relieving her of the immediate anxiety that he might be expecting a more intimate demonstration of commitment from the woman he had just agreed to marry.

Midway through the journey he changed his mind about their destination. Her mother was with her father at the hospital, and the limousine headed there instead.

'The sooner we tell your parents the better. Your father will have less to worry about,' he stated confidently.

Caroline was mortified when her mother reacted with unconcealed delight to their announcement. Wealth evidently cancelled out all

Isabel's former objections to Valente. Caroline could not bring herself to look at Valente, but the look of acceptance and relief in her father's shadowed eyes reinforced her belief that what she was doing was right in so far as it affected her family and the business. Beyond that level she refused to think.

On the way back to Winterwood, Valente discussed his plans for the house and the provision being made for a self-contained apartment on the ground floor which would be adapted to suit her parents' needs. 'They will, of course, be free to use the rest of the house when we're not there.'

'Where will we be?'

'We'll be based in Venice, but I inherited other properties from my grandfather.'

'I didn't know you had a grandfather alive—or one rich enough to own properties in the plural,' she confided in great surprise.

'I'll fill you in some time.' Valente lifted an almost languid hand and gently tucked a stray strand of pale hair back behind her ear. Brilliant dark eyes welded to her, he slowly lowered his handsome dark head. She stayed still and shut her eyes tight, a restive heat curling between her thighs, heightening her awareness. He brushed his lips slowly back and forth over hers and she quivered, parting her lips for him, curious rather than scared.

'I want you very much, *belleza mia*. Tell your mother I won't wait for a big fancy wedding. Assure her that I will cover any bill, no matter how outrageous, but that it has to take place within the next two weeks. My staff will assist.' He dipped his tongue sensuously slowly into the tender interior of her mouth.

'Two…weeks?' Caroline gasped, jerking her head away. 'Are you crazy?'

'Impatient. I'll apply for a special licence,' Valente traded huskily, long fingers closing to her chin to steady her for a slow, deep kiss that went on for so long she felt dizzy. She marvelled that she liked his mouth on hers, the light pressure, the subtle seduction of his tongue, and she was also terrifyingly conscious of the hand he had braced on her thigh, of how easily he might push up her dress to access more intimate places. At the very thought of that, she tensed.

'Of course there's no reason why we should wait to share a bed, *gioia mia*,' he added as he straightened and lifted his hand from her thigh. 'But you want me to wait, don't you?'

Her nerves as tight as piano wires, Caroline whispered shakily, 'Yes…yes, I do.'

'I've waited so long already, *belleza mia*. I'll keep you in bed for a month when I finally get you there,' he promised thickly.

And anguish washed through her, for she knew that he would soon be disillusioned and that he would hate her. She remembered how, five years earlier, she had once innocently longed for his lovemaking, even while holding back out of the fear that sex might be all he wanted from her. Shy though she had been, however, she had wanted that final intimacy and had never feared his passion. She'd had complete faith in him—a faith that had proved as reliable as shifting sand when it was challenged by others. That weakness was her fatal flaw, and telling Valente how afraid she had been back then that marrying him would be a bad mistake would only infuriate him. Then he would leave her, and she would lose him all over again. Her parents would be homeless, Hales Transport would close down, and her father would have to wait a long time for his surgery. Either way, no matter what she did, she would be responsible for everything that went wrong. He had said he admired loyalty. How much would he admire hers when she cheated him for the benefit of her family?

'What's up?' Valente demanded, recognising the strain pinching her profile into tightness.

'Nothing's up.'

Caroline twisted to look at him. The moonlight arrowing into the back of the luxury car accentuated the strong angles and defined hollows of his hard handsome features. For the first time in more years than she wanted to remember she wanted to make physical contact with a man of her own volition. She wanted to smooth that aggressive jawline already roughening with stubble, trace that arrogant Roman emperor's nose and that beautiful, brutally stubborn mouth. Without warning, as her tense fingers quivered with longing, it hit her like a tidal wave that the very idea of admitting her sexual inadequacy and watching Valente turn away from her in angry disgust was altogether more than she could bear. Fear of the future swiftly formed a cold hard knot inside her.

Joe Hales stared as Caroline descended the stairs in her wedding dress. It was a classic design, chosen because it would not swamp her small frame in an excess of fabric. Her gown had jewelled straps on the shoulders, and it fitted her like a glove to below the hip, where it flared into a fuller skirt. She wore a short veil, held by a silver tiara on top of her upswept hair.

'You look as pretty as a picture,' her father told her proudly, his eyes glassy with tears. 'I don't understand why your mother thought that you wearing a proper wedding gown would be in bad taste.'

'Matthew,' his daughter proffered, in one succinct word of explanation. 'But, as you know, Valente wanted me to wear a gown.'

The older man's eyes crinkled at the corners with wry amusement. 'Your mother doesn't like to be contradicted.'

'Neither does he,' Caroline remarked ruefully, thinking of the various tussles there had been over such decisions during the past two weeks, not to mention the outraged descent of Matt's parents when they realised she was re-marrying. Caroline had chosen to withstand the older couple's condemnation with dignified understanding, but her mother had not been so tolerant of their interference.

Valente, unfortunately, was no more tolerant of views other than his own. He was determined to behave as if her first marriage had never happened, and had swiftly vetoed the suggestion of a civil ceremony with Caroline dressed in a suit in a pastel shade. On several occasions Caroline had been put in the thankless position of playing piggy in the middle between Valente and Isabel, who had craved more time in which to turn her daughter's second wedding into the flashiest in local living memory. Never in her life before had Caroline been kept so relentlessly busy.

Valente had returned to Italy within days of agreeing to marry her, and he had ruled her by phone ever since, reeling off commands as if she was an employee rather than his bride-to-be. Almost all her possessions, including the contents of her workshop, had already been professionally packed and sent off to Venice. Her mother had wanted to stage an evening party after the wedding, but Valente had insisted that the bride and groom would be leaving in the afternoon for Italy. Koko, duly micro-chipped and inoculated for her travels, had been flown out in advance that very morning to Valente's home.

Hales Transport was still in business, and a new warehouse was being commissioned—a comforting sign of an anticipated expansion in trade. In the same two-week period complex alterations to Winterwood had been agreed, after

a lengthy meeting with an architect and her
parents, who had had considerable input into
the design of their new apartment. Joe and
Isabel were overjoyed to be staying on at Winterwood, and delighted by the prospect of a
modern and easily-maintained home. While the
work on the house was being done they would
be staying in a comfortable hotel at Valente's
expense. He had also instructed his staff to
rehire their former housekeeper and gardener to
take care of the property in the Haleses'
absence. As a final footnote to the speed and ef-
fectiveness of Valente's virtual takeover of all
their lives, her father was now scheduled for
surgery at a private hospital the following
month—Valente would be footing the bill.

The pre-nuptial agreement Caroline had
had to sign had been rigorous in its detail. It
had shocked her, covering as it did everything
from infidelity to her allowance and the
amount of travelling she would be allowed to
do. If they had a child she would have to
continue living in Italy even if the marriage
ended in divorce. Every sin she might commit
would affect the size of her divorce settlement, which was set for an amazing amount
of cash. She had signed without arguing a

single clause. If Valente honoured the promises he had already made, she expected nothing more from him.

But now that the wedding was upon her Caroline was as jumpy as a cat on hot bricks during the drive to the church. It was the same church at which she had failed to show up five years before. Valente had refused the suggestion that another venue might be preferable. A red carpet ran down the steps—probably one of the many 'extras' which Valente's staff had organised. Photographs were taken as she entered the old building. She could not shake a daunting sense of déjà vu, because for years she had wondered what her life would have been like had she married Valente instead.

Glorious flowers embellished almost every visible inch of the rather austere interior of the church. She repressed the memories of her first wedding day, during which Matthew had begun to show his true colours. But Valente was not Matthew, she reminded herself furiously, striving to rouse herself and maintain an upbeat mood. Valente turned from the altar to look at her and all her anxiety momentarily died away. He looked gorgeous in his elegant grey morning suit, and his stunning dark golden eyes rested on her with an unconcealed appreciation that lit her up inside with relief and pleasure.

A little voice in her head whispered that he would not be feeling so generous by the end of the day, and even before she silenced that warning voice a shiver of premonition ran down her taut spine like a trickle of icy water. Valente might want her in a way that Matthew had not, but his desire would destroy their marriage before it even got off the ground.

The service was short and sweet. Valente held her hand firmly, slotting a wedding ring smoothly on to her finger. When they were pronounced man and wife, and he turned her round to kiss her, she was startled by the sudden intimacy, the crashing reminder that her body was no longer inviolable.

'Your skin has turned to ice,' Valente remarked half under his breath. 'You must be cold, *belleza mia.*'

But she had only frozen when his mouth had come down hungrily on hers and the fear of how they would fare later that day had exploded back into her with double strength, making her skin clammy. She would not be his 'beauty' then, would she?

'You look amazing, though. Who chose the dress?'

'I did,' she admitted with quiet pride. 'Mum's much too fond of frills and bows.'

Valente bent his handsome dark head lower and murmured huskily, 'I'm especially fond of lace.'

Her pale skin washed tomato-red as that could only be a reminder of the distinctly intimate gift he had had delivered to her the day before. A set of ivory lingerie in silk and lace such as she had never seen before and certainly never worn: a cobweb-fine bra and knickers, teamed with a suspender belt and lace stockings and the all-essential bridal garter. She had felt quite sick looking at the set, even more intimidated when she'd forced herself to put the items on to wear below her dress. After all, no gift could have told her more candidly exactly what her bridegroom expected from her.

He wanted a fantasy woman who would parade half-naked for his enjoyment and be bold and adventurous in his bed. He had built her up in his mind into more than she felt she could ever be. A woman confident of her perfect body and her sexuality would enjoy wearing such lingerie to excite her man. But Caroline was afraid of male excitement, and all too well aware of her physical flaws, of her small breasts and slim hips that carried not a hint of the voluptuous femininity that so many men preferred.

'You look like an ice queen… Smile,' Valente instructed on the steps of the church, while his security men kept a bunch of photographers behind barriers. A crowd of journalists were shouting questions in a foreign language.

'Why are all these reporters so interested in us?' Caroline whispered. 'Are they foreign?'

'Italian. I'm very well known at home,' he returned casually. 'And my bride is naturally a source of interest as well.'

The reception was to be held at the same hotel where Valente had stayed. His physical reserve with her was fading fast by the time they got there, and the change in him sent her nervous tension rocketing. Her brain told her that he was now quite naturally treating her like a wife as he put an arm round her and drew her close, or when he covered her hand with his, or took her on to the dance floor and welded her so close to him it was a challenge for her to breathe. Sealed by the slow pace of the music to his lean, powerful frame, she became inordinately aware of his masculine response to their proximity.

'I'm counting the hours until we're alone together, *cara mia*,' he imparted in a roughened whisper that sent her heart hammering into an all-out sprint. 'All day we've been surrounded by people.'

'Yes,' she responded dry-mouthed, dreading the instant when she could no longer hide behind the presence of others.

He covered her champagne flute with his hand when a waiter attempted to top it up. 'I want my bride wide awake,' he teased, and she tried to produce a laugh and failed abysmally.

'I don't have a problem with alcohol,' she whispered.

'But you certainly do have a problem with food,' Valente countered, taking her aback with that incisive comment. 'You play with it but you never seem to eat it.'

'I lose my appetite when I'm nervous… that's all.'

'What do you have to be so nervous about?'

'Well, your guest-list for a start. There are some very important people here,' Caroline pointed out, desperate to provide a credible excuse for her nerves.

Valente's impressive guests ranged from Italian politicians and powerful international businessmen to a surprising bunch of very toffee-nosed cousins, who were behaving like aristocrats being forced to socialise with the lower classes. When she had asked him who they were and where they appeared on what he had once assured her was a very humble family tree, he had shrugged and given her no definitive explanation.

'Don't let anyone make you feel uncomfortable, *tesora mia*. This is your day. You are the most important person here,' Valente had responded instead.

But Caroline felt more like a fake and a cheat, and her frame of mind was not improved by her mother's comments while she was changing out of her dress into the sapphire-blue shift and beaded jacket that comprised her going-away outfit.

'Just think,' Isabel Hales urged. 'You turned Valente down five years ago and inspired him into making a fortune so that he could come back and claim you!'

Caroline winced. 'It wasn't like that at all. I didn't turn up at the church then and I let him down badly.'

'But that wasn't your fault—'

Five years ago Valente loved me, she wanted

to scream. But now she meant nothing more to
him than a long-awaited sexual experience. And
in that context she certainly would be new and
different, she conceded painfully.

Shortly after his private jet took off Valente
rested questioning ebony eyes on her and
breathed, 'What's the matter with you?'

Taken by surprise, Caroline blinked in confusion. 'What do you mean?'

'It's like someone has sucked all the life out
of you,' he imparted with frowning force, releasing his belt to stand up. 'You've turned into the
original walking, talking doll since we came
out of that church this morning.'

Intimidated by his attitude, Caroline shrank
back into her opulent leather seat. 'It's been a
stressful couple of weeks…'

'*Per meraviglia!* It was your wedding day!'
Valente retorted in a crushing tone of exasperation. 'Isn't this what you wanted? Marriage and
all the frills?'

Caroline was so tense that she was almost hy-
perventilating, and her heart was thundering in
her ears. She got his point—she really did! She
had insisted on marriage when he hadn't
wanted it, but he had still laid on all the bridal

trimmings and acted the part of gracious bridegroom. A walking, talking doll. She recognised
that it was a cruelly apt label for her stiff reserve
so far today. Although in some ways he did not
know her at all, he nonetheless knew her well
enough to know that something was badly
wrong. But there was no easy way of telling her
new husband it was fear of the wedding night
he was looking forward to that was at the base
of her strained behaviour. For an instant she
toyed with the idea of telling him the truth, but
then, just at that moment, one of the cabin crew
entered with a trolley and she lost her nerve.

'I think I'm a bit tired,' she muttered apolo-
getically, and it was not a lie for she had barely
slept for several nights.

That plausible explanation made Valente's
brow clear and his tension evaporated. He
smiled down at her before reaching down to
unclip her seat belt and scoop her up easily into
his arms. 'You should try to get some sleep
during the flight.'

He set her down in the sleeping compartment
and helped her out of her jacket. Everything he
did simply unnerved her and, pausing only to
kick off her shoes, she lay down still in her
dress, her lashes screening her anxious eyes.

'Wouldn't you be more comfortable without your dress?' Valente asked in surprise.

'I'm fine like this,' she told him, only breathing again once the door had closed firmly on his exit. Then she lay sleepless, staring up at the ceiling and wondering what on earth she was going to do…

CHAPTER SEVEN

UNTIL they landed in Tuscany Caroline had assumed their destination was Venice. Now they were driving through rolling woodland with glimpses of hilltop villages and serried ranks of grapevines illuminated by the setting sun. It was a gorgeous landscape. Finally she surrendered to her curiosity.

'Where are we going?'

'The Villa Barbieri, left to me by my grandfather, Ettore.'

'When did he die?'

'Three years ago.'

'You must have been close?' she assumed.

'No, not in the cosy sense that you mean. But although we had very little in common aside from the blood in our veins, we understood each other very well,' Valente pronounced coolly.

Caroline was wholly unprepared for the long gravelled drive lined with tall cypresses that led up to the most huge and magnificent house, fronted by a massive portico that would not have shamed a palace. 'My word,' she mumbled, wide-eyed. 'Who *was* your grandfather?'

'He was a count, with a dozen other lesser titles and a pedigree that stretched back to the Middle Ages. A man of great pride and intelligence who only chose to acknowledge my existence after the rest of his family had bled him dry.'

'That sounds like a fascinating story.'

'But not one I want to share, *piccola mia*. Content yourself with the knowledge that your mother will be ecstatic when you send her a photo and mention my connection to the aristocracy.'

Caroline reddened as though she had been slapped, but she could not argue with his forecast. Her mother's great reverence for social status and wealth was as well known as it was embarrassing.

Valente led her into the enormous house, past alcoves adorned with marble statues and a parade of huge oil paintings. They were greeted in a great circular hall by a bowing rotund older man and a long line of staff.

'The head of the household—the irre-placeable Umberto,' Valente quipped with a smile as the older man stepped forward.

Caroline was so shocked by what she was discovering about Valente's life in Italy that even though Umberto addressed her in English she could barely manage to string two words together. Five years earlier Valente had described the tiny Venetian apartment where he lived—the lack of modern facilities, the regular flooding and damp. Yet now it seemed that Valente was living like royalty. Her one-time frog had become a prince, only she doubted that a fairytale ending was in store for him or her.

Her tension broke when a familiar, dainty, furry figure came bounding out of a room nearby. 'Koko…' Caroline exclaimed in unconcealed delight, the familiar sight of her pet never more welcome.

Giving the distinctive cries with which she communicated, the Siamese cat wound her slender graceful body affectionately round Caroline's ankles before condescending to be lifted and stroked, Valente came close to inspect the little animal. Koko's round blue eyes blazed, the hair on her little head puffing up in an aggressive display as she spat and hissed at him, baring her teeth.

'No, Koko,' Caroline scolded, adding without thought, 'She never took to Matthew either.'

The hardening of Valente's jawline warned her that that had been a tactless reference.

An evening meal awaited them in a dining room as large and imposing as might have been expected in a building where the hall was big enough to function as a soldiers' parade ground. While they were served exquisitely cooked and presented food Koko sat at her feet, releasing plaintive cries until Caroline let her pet curl up on her lap.

'That is a spoilt cat,' Valente commented.

'Probably, but I'm very attached to her,' Caroline admitted, thinking of how often the little animal had mirrored her mood and provided her with company and affection when she was feeling low.

Now, conscious that Valente noticed when she didn't eat, Caroline made a real effort to rescue her appetite and consume a reasonable amount of what was put in front of her. It troubled her, though, that she was already trying to please Valente, just as she had once tried and failed to please Matthew. Would there ever come a time when she could simply please herself? When dinner was over, Valente addressed Umberto in Italian and swept her up the superb marble cantilevered staircase.

'This is your room,' he announced, closing the door in Koko's face before the cat could cross the threshold, making it clear that there were boundaries to his tolerance. The large bedroom was furnished with polished antiques and ornamented with splendid flower arrangements. He pressed open doors, showing her the *en-suite* bathroom and then a dressing room before opening a third and final door. 'This is my room. I like my own space, *piccola mia.*'

Frozen in the middle of the room, Caroline felt more rejected than comforted by that information. It reminded her that he had not wanted to marry her, that she had forced that issue, and that presumably he carried a certain amount of resentment over that fact. It was a suspicion that could only made her shiver. She did not want to go to bed with a man in a bad mood.

A knock sounded on the door and Valente opened it. Umberto entered with champagne and deftly poured the golden liquid into a pair of flutes, while the funereal silence rubbed Caroline's nerves even rawer than they already were.

'Not for me,' she breathed when Valente extended her glass, for she was afraid that in the over-hyped state she was in the alcohol might make her sick.

Valente took only a sip from his own flute before drawing her to him with slow, steady hands and a dark glow of warmth in his gaze that made her tummy flip. 'Now, show me how to enjoy being married,' he urged.

It was an invitation that not unnaturally deprived her of speech—and then the force of her feverish tension blew a hole in her armour. 'I'm going to disappoint you,' she told him abruptly.

'That would be impossible,' Valente contradicted instantly in his dark accented drawl, sliding her jacket off her shoulders so smoothly that she didn't know it was gone until he set it aside. He turned her round as though she was indeed that doll he had compared her to earlier, and ran down the zip on her dress. He pressed his lips to a slight smooth shoulder and the dress fell.

Caroline stepped out of it, terrifyingly aware of how sexually inviting she had to look in the scanty lingerie he had given her. She heard him expel his breath on a slow hiss of appreciation. 'You look fantastic.'

'Just like a fantasy?' she pressed unevenly.

One lean hand closing over her limp fingers, he spun her round, smouldering black-lashed golden eyes wandering from the pert tilt of her breasts encased in ivory satin to the lace stockings that encased her long slender legs. '*Si*... I can hardly believe that I finally have you here with me, *belezza mia*.'

He brought his wide, sensual mouth hungrily down on hers. He played with her pouting lower lip and let his tongue dart skilfully beyond. He tasted her with slow deep hunger and she quivered, afraid of his passion and his strength but fighting the fear with all her might. He caught her up unexpectedly in his arms and carried her over to the big bed. Her imagination immediately leapt ahead to the mortification of nakedness awaiting her, the pain and the resentment.

Valente settled shrewd dark eyes on her. Her rigid position on the bed made him think of a doe looking down a double-barrelled shotgun, and he frowned at that illogical image. But there was no denying that Caroline's behaviour never quite added up in the way he expected. ESP was still sending him messages he could not interpret. She had wanted this marriage, had fought for it. Yet, for a gold-digger, she had put up a very poor fight before she signed the prenuptial agreement without protesting a single clause. His lawyers had been ecstatic, and had

assured him that his wealth was ring-fenced for
eternity as far as she was concerned. Money
evidently wasn't what turned her on most. But
if it was social status he now had plenty of that
as well, so what was wrong with her?

She was shy, she had always been shy, and
she was a little nervous, he reasoned while
he shed his jacket, tie and shoes. A woman
who had been married for almost four years
shouldn't be *that* nervous, though, should she?

Caroline fought to keep her breathing even.
She was so worked up she wanted to gasp. But
she was going to lie back and think of England,
as no doubt countless women had over the cen-
turies. Enjoyment wasn't even on the cards. But
it was going to work with him, it was going to
work, she told herself over and over again. She
took off her shoes and scrambled below the
linen sheet while wondering what he would say
if she asked him to turn the lights out. Then she
finally looked at him as he was ditching his silk
boxers and gulped, shocked by the awesome
size of his erection, thinking that no, no way
would she be able to give him what he wanted.

She was as pale as marble and as still, Valente
reflected, dark brows pleated in bewilderment.
Willing? Unwilling? Odd how it had never

occurred to him that she might genuinely not want him. Was he so vain that he had refused even to acknowledge that possibility? But he had felt the buzz between them again, just as he had five years earlier, the unmistakable reciprocal pulse of sexual desire. Reassured by that conviction, Valente lowered himself down on the bed beside her, six foot plus of daunting masculinity and potency. He let his lean sun-bronzed body lightly connect with hers while he kissed her. And she liked the kiss, in fact she loved the kiss, and a little sound of pleasure escaped her. But then she felt the pulse of his arousal against her thigh, and the loosening of her bra as he released the fastening. It was too much too soon, and panic threatened to take her over.

Matthew's taunts flooded her mind, and she cringed as a lean hand closed over one tiny mound and a thumb massaged the delicate bud of her nipple. A sort of tingling sensation ran through her, like a sting, and she froze, instinct taking over as she steeled herself for at best discomfort and at worst pain.

'Your breasts are so beautiful, *belezza mia*,' Valente breathed huskily, admiring the porcelain-fine skin of the pouting flesh and the nipple as delicate as a pale pink flower. He lowered his arrogant dark head to explore that sweet flesh with his mouth.

Caroline could not stop herself from raising her hands to push at his shoulders, wide fearful eyes pinned to him. 'Please don't….'

Astonishment stilled Valente in his tracks. 'You don't like that? *Bene*…it's not a problem.'

Caroline shut her eyes tight and dragged in a sustaining breath. Of course it was a problem—everythin*g* she was feeling was a problem! His hand was on her thigh and she went rigid, a cold chill spreading through her lower limbs from deep inside her. He wasn't hurting her, he wasn't hurting her, she reminded herself fiercely, fighting her apprehension with every atom of her strength, but still she trembled.

In the lamplight, Valente studied her in ferocious confusion. Not only was she pale as marble, she was as unresponsive. He could feel the clamminess of her skin, her mental withdrawal. He had never met with such a reaction from a woman before, and her obvious distress pierced his ego like a knife plunging into his gut. 'What's wrong?' he demanded grittily. 'Where are you in all this? This is our wedding night, but you're making me feel like a rapist.'

Her feathery lashes lifted. 'I'm sorry…I'm just nervous.'

She didn't want him. *She didn't want him.* Valente looked into the misty depths of her grey eyes and willed her to prove otherwise, but neither encouragement nor even recognition energised her blank defensive expression. She didn't want him. *He* didn't want to accept that possibility. He lifted one hand and buried it in the tumble of her silvery blonde hair, cupping her small head with the span of his hand, holding her steady as he brought his sensual mouth back down on hers with all the demanding hunger he had until that moment controlled.

Taking fright at that forcefulness, and feeling trapped, Caroline reacted instinctively, tearing free of him and throwing herself backwards across the bed to slither down onto the floor. She braced her hands on the mattress for an instant before she straightened, because she was dizzy with stress and fear. 'I can't….I just can't do this with you!'

His darkly handsome features stamped with stunned disbelief, Valente thrust back the bedding and sprang upright. Hugging herself tight with defensive arms, Caroline watched him pull on his boxers. The raw tension in his handsome, dark profile and broad, bronzed shoulders was powerfully apparent to her assessing, anxious gaze. Once again she had upset and hurt him. She felt as if she was bleeding inside and she hated herself.

Valente swung round to settle shimmering golden eyes on her like metal grappling hooks. 'What the hell is going on here? You wanted me to marry you—'

'I know…I know. I'm sorry—'

'Sorry doesn't cut it in this scenario,' Valente incised. 'I want an explanation.'

Her troubled eyes strayed down over his lean, powerful physique and veered away when she realised that the silk boxers could not conceal the bold bulge of his arousal. Guilt assailed her in a choking tide. 'I told you I was no good at sex…'

'What just happened in that bed was about more than you not being good at sex,' Valente flung back at her in condemnation. 'You turned into a marble statue in my arms, and then you fought free of my arms as if you were being assaulted!'

'I thought it might be different with you… I'm so sorry.' Caroline was fighting the buckets of overwrought tears penned up behind her eyes, determined not to stoop to that very feminine plea for sympathy. 'I couldn't bear it.'

That last phrase was all Valente absorbed: *I couldn't bear it.* 'It' being his touch and proximity. Dark blood settled over his stunning cheekbones and a shudder rippled through his big body, and coiling his masculine hands into powerful fists.

'Then why did you marry me?' he demanded rawly.

Feeling all the more naked and foolish, standing there in front of him with her arms crossed in a protective screen over her breasts, Caroline said, 'I want to get dressed and then we can…talk.'

'*Maledizione*…you will talk now,' Valente delivered with emphatic force. 'I have listened to enough nonsense.'

Caroline took him by surprise and backed into the bathroom to her right, slamming shut the door and ramming home the bolt to lock it with trembling urgency. That achieved, she stripped off what remained of the fancy lingerie with frantic hands. She hated those fanciful undergarments which could only remind her of her inadequacies in the seduction field.

'I'm out of patience. If you don't come out,

I'll kick the door down,' Valente warned her dangerously from the other side of the door.

Caroline grabbed the flamboyant turquoise silk robe that hung on the back of the door and put it on. It had been made for someone a good deal taller and carried the exotic scent of another woman's perfume. Of course he had had other lovers—probably hundreds of them, she thought wildly, and every one of them would have given him more pleasure than she ever could. As the door was struck with savage force she looked desperately round the tiled room for some means of escape, but she was stuck. The bolt broke away from the wood on the second blow and the door swung wide.

Valente focused on her standing there, as straight and defiant as an early Christian martyr while wrapped in his former mistress's robe. As a picture it was all wrong. Housekeeping, he acknowledged, had fallen down in not removing that garment. It was not a moment when he wanted to be reminded of Agnese's voluptuous sensuality in the bedroom. Agnese, who hadn't been able to get enough of him between the sheets. Agnese, who had begged him to keep her on even after his marriage and who had dared to suggest that no wife could replace her.

And just this once, Agnese, whose beauty and vanity were legendary, had been proved right.

'How dare you do that to me…?' Caroline protested, trembling like a leaf after that demonstration of male aggression. She felt helpless, threatened, for she did not know how to defuse his anger.

'How dare *you* pose there, shaking like I'm about to physically hurt you?' Valente raked back at her, closing a firm hand round her wrist and urging her back into the bedroom. 'I'm entitled to an explanation from you. Feeling like you obviously do about me, why did you insist on marrying me?'

It was the question she had most dreaded, for she could not defend herself on that score. 'I couldn't have cut it as a mistress,' she pointed out heavily, half under her breath. 'You wouldn't have helped my parents or Hales after an experience like this. So it had to be marriage. That's your fault. You offered me so much to be with you that you made it impossible for me to refuse.'

Outraged condemnation had fired his beautiful eyes to a golden heat that threatened to burn her tender skin. 'Yet right from the beginning you knew that the only thing I wanted from you was sex. So you deliberately set out to rip me off.'

Caroline tore her guilty gaze from him and studied the carpet. 'There wasn't a choice. But I did hope it would work out between us.'

'Even though you recoiled from me in disgust the first time we kissed again?' he bit out rawly.

Caroline paled. 'That's not what I felt.'

'How could you possibly have hoped it would work out? I was so hot for you I was blind to all the signals that something was wrong and you knew it. You kept your distance and played me right up to the doors of the church. You're a liar and a fraud!'

Every word cut into her like a knife, reminding her of failings that she was already all too well aware of. 'Yes, in that field I was…but I did try to tell you the truth about me at the beginning,' she reminded him painfully, the intimate conversation tearing off entire layers off her protective skin. Now that he knew her secret, she felt horribly exposed. 'I'm frigid. It's my problem, nothing to do with you.'

'*Dannazione!* How can it be nothing to do with me? You promised to give me a child. What hope have we now of achieving that ambition?'

Caroline was pale as milk. 'None, I suppose.'

'You cheated me, and I don't allow anyone who does that to walk away unscathed. You may be my wife, but for how much longer?' Valente slung that question at her with icy derision. 'You left one salient fact out of your financial calculations. If this marriage isn't consummated I can have it set aside and it will be as if we were never married. I'll be free of you and you will no longer be entitled to a settlement of any kind.'

With that final contemptuous speech Valente snatched up the clothing he had discarded, strode into the adjoining bedroom and closed the door firmly in his wake.

What shook Caroline at that instant was that she had to stop herself from running after him. What shook her even more was the intense emotional pain of his rejection. He hated her. He couldn't wait to get rid of her. It was as if the roof had fallen in above her and the floor beneath her feet had vanished, so that she was still falling, falling, falling, in a never-ending downward spiral. *The only thing I wanted from you was sex.* And it was the one thing she couldn't give him.

The veil between her plotting and her secret desires had been torn apart by their confrontation. Had she wed him for her family's sake? To save the workers at Hales from the dole queue?

Or because she had dreamt of turning the clock back five years and magically reclaiming the love she had once lost? Wasn't it true that what she had really wanted more than anything else was a second chance with Valente? But history was history, and couldn't be eradicated any more than she could get over her sexual dysfunction just because she wanted to. In despair, she sobbed into the pillow.

Even though it was late, Valente wanted to phone his legal team and put them to work on ridding him of his brand-new wife. Having switched off his emotions, he was in business mode, and keen to take action on what he viewed as an act of fraud committed against him. But the prospect of telling anyone alive that his bride had just refused him froze him into rare inactivity. Dressed, he strode downstairs, startling the staff still engaged on cleaning the dining room. He poured a drink in the drawing room and strode out on to the loggia.

I thought it might be different with you. Her words fluttered back to haunt his disarranged thoughts. It had been that bad with Matthew, as well? Valente's rage began to abate at that awareness. She didn't like sex, and whose fault was that? It was a fault that could only be laid at Matthew Bailey's door. Pacing the loggia, while Umberto lit candles on the stone tables and sent his employer concerned glances, Valente pieced back together everything he knew about his bride.

Five years back she had been shy, innocent and inhibited, but she had never shown the slightest hint of fear when he touched her. There had been nothing abnormal about her reactions. Could he have been mistaken about the response she had recently given him when he kissed her? Was she repelled by him personally? Or simply repelled by sex? And what did the fear and her flight into the bathroom to shelter behind a locked door suggest? A fear that he might not take no for an answer? The lean strong bones of his face clenched hard on that suspicion. The instant he acknowledged her terror, everything else fell into place. She had had to get drunk to come to him at the hotel that night. She had been miserable throughout their wedding day out of fear of what the night would bring.

Without a doubt she had known she had a serious problem, and she hadn't shared it because she had been afraid he would walk away, when he was the only guy available to solve all her family problems. While he understood, he couldn't forgive her for her deception. Nothing could excuse her trickery in demanding a role she could not fulfil. And she still owed him answers.

When Valente entered the bedroom without warning, Caroline slowly lifted her dismayed face from the crumpled pillow. She had never looked plainer. Her hair was a mess, her nose red and her eyes badly swollen. But, oddly enough, her obvious distress soothed Valente, who decided she had rarely looked so appealing. Koko, clearly having triumphed over the bedroom ban, was curled up against her mistress like a Siamese second skin.

'Why…er…what do you want?' Caroline prompted tautly.

Valente scooped up the cat, strode back to the door and deposited the outraged and hissing cat back out into the corridor—but not before he had fallen victim to the lightning-fast slash of a punitive little claw across the back of his hand.

'She's welcome everywhere else but not in the bedrooms,' Valente announced, while

Caroline studied him as though he had taken a whip to her pet.

'If you've got anything else to say to me, couldn't it wait until tomorrow?' she asked.

'No, it couldn't. I've had a lousy wedding day and an even lousier wedding night. I want to know what turned you off sex.'

'No! I couldn't possibly discuss something so private with you,' Caroline argued in open consternation.

Brilliant eyes dark as ebony, and hard as diamonds in the lamplight, Valente sat down on the edge of the bed. 'Well, the only other option is for you to discuss the problem with a stranger—a sex therapist.'

Her grey eyes widened, her horror unhidden in the face of what clearly struck her as an even greater challenge.

His sardonic mouth curled. 'I win by default? Even though a counsellor could be just what you need.'

'I just don't want to talk about it,' she breathed painfully.

Valente threw his broad shoulders back against the pillows. 'Tough.'

'What are you doing?' she gasped, unnerved by his presence back on the bed.

'Getting comfortable.' Without a hint of awkwardness, Valente punched the pillows into shape and settled lithely back against them, his long, lean body assuming a relaxed sprawl that mocked her seething tension. 'Tell me what your last wedding night was like…'

Caroline stiffened, and what colour there was in her cheeks drained away.

In the crushing silence that clawed at her already ragged nerves, Valente rested his shrewd gaze on her only for a moment. He was well aware that he had chosen a vulnerable time to stage his grilling, but equally aware that he was more likely to get the truth out of her. 'Were you intimate with him before the wedding?'

Caroline shook her head in a silent negative. During those fraught weeks between inadvertently jilting Valente and agreeing to marry Matthew she had rarely been alone with her bridegroom. 'He didn't seem interested,' she confided flatly. 'Although I didn't appreciate it at the time, he married me for the business and for the promise he'd be put in charge of it. I was very stupid. I just took it for granted that the private stuff would fall into place. We were married before I realised that I wasn't the sort of woman he had ever found attractive.'

'How did you find that out?'

Caroline lay as still as if she was made of solid stone and studied the ceiling, her hands clasped taut, fingernails biting crescents into her tender skin. 'He was drunk on our wedding night… He—' her voice sank even lower '—he made a lot of jokes about how flat-chested and boyish my body was.'

Tensing at that startling admission, Valente almost groaned his disbelief out loud. 'Go on…'

'He got angry with me when I couldn't respond the way he wanted. He drank a lot and he got rough and he hurt me,' she muttered in an anguished rush of embarrassment. 'Then he lost interest. Of course he tried a few other times, and every time it didn't work he got angrier with me. He said I'd made him impotent and he started sleeping in the room next door.'

Shattered by what he was finding out, Valente breathed, 'So when did you finally manage to consummate your marriage?'

Caroline swallowed hard. 'We…didn't. He had an affair with a woman who was much more his style than I was. He liked to tell me about her—'

Black brows drawing together at the full cat-astrophic truth of the abusive relationship she had suffered with Bailey, Valente leant closer, his lean, muscular frame very tense. 'Are you telling me that you never had sex with him?'

In squirming mortification Caroline rolled over, presenting a defensive back to him. 'After the first three months he never came near me again. He kept up a front around his parents because we lived with them. Luckily it was a very big house. Matt acted like I didn't exist most of the time.'

Valente rolled her back, so that he could look at her pale heart-shaped face and defeated gaze. Luxuriant jet-dark lashes low over shimmering golden eyes, he breathed huskily, 'You're still a virgin?'

'What does that have to do with anything?' she almost spat at him, in angry embarrassment over the extent of his probing.

'It means a great deal to me, *belleza mia*. It means I'm getting back what I believed had been stolen from me,' Valente confessed candidly, all his tension evaporating. 'What else did he do to you? Did he knock you about?'

'No, he only ever hit me once…when he discovered that I'd searched your name on the internet.'

Valente was appalled. He went from being

boyishly pleased that she had sought information about him to being sobered by the price she had paid for her curiosity.

'It's time we got some sleep,' Valente murmured flatly.

'We?' she queried anxiously.

'*Si*…sleeping apart will only divide us more. I promise that I won't do anything you don't want. I also assure you that I won't get angry, I will never be rough, and I will never, ever hurt you.' Valente intoned those promises steadily, in his dark, distinctive drawl.

'Or force me to do anything I don't want to do?' she pressed.

Valente set his even white teeth together so hard he almost chipped them. It was well for Matthew Bailey that he was safely dead and buried, for Valente had long loathed men who abused women. 'Of course not. You must learn to trust me.'

'That's so hard,' she admitted, watching him stride into the dressing room, listening to doors being opened and shut.

Valente emerged with a handful of burgundy-coloured silk which he tossed on the bed. 'I bought you a new wardrobe as a wedding present. Change out of that robe.'

'Who does it belong to?' she asked, with a piercing sensation in her chest.

'Nobody you need to consider.'

Valente was reflecting that he had always enjoyed a challenge, that nothing he had ever gained had been easily acquired. On the other hand, she had chosen to marry that bastard Matthew, and Valente was not prepared to wait for ever to enjoy the delights of what should have been his. The ache at his groin reminded him that celibacy had never agreed with him, either. Patience promised to be a gruelling challenge.

Too exhausted to protest, Caroline went into the bathroom. There she shed the robe that she guessed had belonged to a former lover and shimmied into the nightdress before scrambling into bed. Valente was getting undressed, and she looked away hurriedly, shrinking from that intimacy.

'I'm not making any other promises, *piccola mia*,' Valente spelt out succinctly. 'Tonight changed everything between us…'

'Yes,' she agreed flatly, refusing to look at him and burrowing below the sheet.

'I'm not a man who makes hasty decisions. I'll give our marriage a chance. We'll move one step at a time.'

Tears seeped out below her tightly shut lashes. She was defective goods, but he would graciously give her a trial before he sent her back to England. Once again a man was ensuring she believed that all she had to offer was her body. Feeling as though he had battered her with his condescension, she closed her eyes tight, praying for sleep to come quickly, for she was beyond even thinking about the future.

But she didn't need to think about it, did she? Inevitably he would divorce her. There was no advantage to him in staying married to a woman like her. She had brought him no business dowry and she could not give him a child. What had happened with Matthew had happened a second time. But this time she was heartbroken, and it was all too easy for her to think of herself as absolutely useless again…

CHAPTER EIGHT

EVERY time she glimpsed the magnificent panoramic outlook from the terrace of the Villa Barbieri, Caroline wondered if she had accidentally strayed into paradise.

It was the most beautiful still day, and she loved the silence. The terracotta roofs of the sleepy village on the hilltop were a charming enhancement to the ancient honey-coloured and much-repaired stone walls of the buildings. The far view of the looming Alps was misty and indistinct, while the lush hills opposite were covered with fresh, green chestnut trees, acacias, scrub oak and broom, before petering out into the fertile valley where silvery-green olive groves and lines of grapevines took over.

She lay in the shade on her stomach, with her bikini top undone and Koko dozing beneath her lounger. If ever a cat had been born to live in a house the size of a palace it was Koko. She might hiss and spit at Valente, and emit noisy, sulky cries from a distance when he was around, but Caroline's pet had wasted no time in making fans of the staff, who could not do enough to make the little cat feel at home.

'She's incredibly jealous of me,' Valente had declared the week before. 'As far as she's concerned, I've stolen her place with you.'

And it was true, Caroline conceded with a wondering smile at that truth. Koko had been banned from the bedroom, while Valente slept with Caroline every night that he was in residence. He was travelling back and forth to Venice, usually only spending one night away from her at most. It hurt that he had never asked her to go with him, but when he was at the Villa Barbieri she woke up in his arms and increasingly fell asleep in them as well. Enclosed in that simple, unthreatening togetherness with a man for the first time, she had gradually learned to trust him. Somehow she had even learned to long for more than his kisses as he controlled his passion while assiduously stoking hers. Step by step, he had promised only four weeks earlier, and she was already becoming unnervingly eager for the next move forward.

From the first, he had encouraged her to touch

him, to explore at will and experiment, and she had soon discovered that the more familiar she became with that lean, beautifully masculine and intensely responsive body of his, the less nervous she was around him. Her fear had gone, for he had proved how self-controlled he could be. With a little sigh she shifted her hips in a sensuous circle on the lounger, recalling how she had wakened him the day before, and the unrestrained sound of his satisfaction while he buried his hands in her hair and urged her on.

With a wicked little quiver of awareness alight low in her belly, she acknowledged that her physical barriers were coming down—and why not? If Valente's wonderful patience with her had taught her anything, it was that he was still the man she had loved when she was twenty-one years old. And at least he was no longer being forced to go without any sexual satisfaction at all, she reflected. Her cheeks hot, she smiled in remembrance of the pleasure she had discovered she could give him. And she had given that pleasure eagerly, while marvelling at the change in herself and the newly learned confidence driving it.

A helicopter flew overhead while she ruminated over the truth that, given time, she was convinced she would be able to meet the terms of their marital agreement. Valente would win where Matthew had failed, which she supposed was only to be expected when she was in love with Valente and desperate to be part of a normal marriage. She had never got over losing Valente, which was hardly surprising in the circumstances. Her horribly ill-judged rebound marriage to Matthew had made it all too clear to her what she had lost… Footsteps sounded on the terrace and she lifted her head.

'I thought you wouldn't be back until late tonight!' Caroline exclaimed, glancing up in surprise and welcome at her tall, well-built husband.

Valente sat down on the lounger beside hers, his lean, darkly handsome features serious. 'Since you're flying back to England to be with your father for his surgery tomorrow, I thought I should finish up early.'

'Good.' Caroline smiled up at him, her entire face lighting up.

Sexual hunger hit Valente as hard as a punch in the stomach. He wanted to haul into his arms and carry her up to bed, but he knew better than to succumb to such a caveman impulse around her. To occupy himself, he leant forward instead and retied the straps on her bikini top. 'Keep the little white patches intact,' he urged softly. 'I find them very sexy, *tesora mia*.'

Caroline sat up, reddening to the roots of her pale hair. The atmosphere was thick with tension. Hot dark golden eyes travelled from her full pink mouth down to the taut little breasts restrained by her bikini top, which she longed for him to uncover. Her mouth ran dry, the hunger in his all-male gaze causing a burst of sudden heat in her pelvis. Her nipples tightened to an almost painful degree. The very knowledge of his desire made her feel dizzy, and somehow proud that she could have that effect on him. Yet she lived in constant fear that frustration would drive him into the arms of another woman before she could get over her hang-ups.

Valente gazed back at her steadily. 'I need a cold shower, or…'

'Or?' she whispered.

'I could take you up to bed and unwrap you and play with you like a toy,' he husked, in a voice laden with lust.

His earthy proposition shocked her, because it was still broad daylight and during those hours they were usually very restrained. The tip of her tongue snaked out to moisten her dry lower lip because she was both seriously tempted and seriously scared that things would go further than she could cope with. 'You won't—?'

'Haven't I proved how good my self-control is yet?'

Having learnt that she got no attention when Valente was around, Koko cried mournfully at the foot of the staircase as Caroline and Valente disappeared from her view.

'That cat is such a bad loser, *belleza mia*,' Valente quipped.

'I bring her up to keep me company when you're not here,' Caroline admitted. 'I suppose it doesn't help that I spoil her.'

'You always had a thing about cats. I remember bringing you little glass cat ornaments back from Venice.'

'I still have them. They're somewhere in the boxes that went to your house in Venice.'

One step inside the doorway of her bedroom, he cupped her cheekbones and kissed her slow and deep, until she was kissing him back and leaning into him, arms stretching up to lock round his neck to keep herself steady. He hoisted her up against him to carry her over to the bed. Although she still seemed to weigh little more than a child, he was satisfied that she was eating more. There was a new, more rounded fullness to her face and her slender limbs. From the bed, she reached up to press the button that closed the curtains.

'Killjoy,' he teased, although the sun was still so bright it pierced through the curtains to illuminate the room.

Still bikini-clad, she scrambled into bed. She knew he liked to undress her and, although she wasn't yet equal to modelling the fantastic collection of lingerie stored in the dressing room, she tried to compensate where she could. Her heart was already thumping as though she had been running. She lay back on the cool linen sheet and watched him remove his business suit. As always, he took her breath away. From his strong brown torso to his long, powerful thighs he was achingly male and extremely sexy. Little quivers of restive warmth were darting through her. She realised in genuine awe that what she was feeling was anticipation.

He slid in beside her. She curved into the heat of him as sinuously as a vine seeking support and parted her full lips for his. She tasted his hunger, the faint tang of wine and the familiar flavour that was uniquely his own. She smiled below the pressure of his mouth when he pressed her flat to the pillows and kissed her long and deep, with more passion than he usually revealed. He had missed her the night before; she was convinced of it, and she really loved that idea.

The bikini top was detached with one gentle tug. Suddenly there was nothing to hide behind any more, and for a split second she lay very still, unable to forget Matthew's taunts. But Valente had already seen her in various states of undress; vanishing into the bathroom every time she needed to change had begun to seem ridiculous. So for him there would be no surprise or disappointment with her body, she reminded herself urgently.

Valente pushed back the sheet and her hands flew up to cover her exposed breasts He made no attempt to stop her but, his dazzling dark eyes intent, studied her through the dense screen of his black lashes and sighed. 'Please let me look at you…'

Feeling foolish, Caroline slowly lowered her palms, and Valente feasted his attention on the pale, pouting perfection of her small breasts. 'You're so beautiful, and you don't even know it because your first husband was an oaf, *gattina mia*.'

Breathing in and out shallowly, Caroline remained still.

'He may not have appreciated you,' Valente breathed, 'but I do…very much.'

He traced the distended length of a swollen pink nipple with his forefinger and she shut her eyes tight and quivered. 'Is that a yes or a no?' he husked.

'Y-yes,' she stammered, weak with longing as the tingle of arousal darted straight down to the pulse already beating between her thighs.

He moulded his hand to one slight mound and she quivered, so innately responsive that she delighted him. He touched her delicate breasts, with the wonderfully lush and prominent nipples she had worked so hard to keep hidden from him, always turning away or covering up the instant she felt his eyes on her. He was as excited as a teenage boy let loose on a woman's body for the first time. He dropped his dark head and let his mouth roam over that silky-soft skin, lingering on her protruding nipples with the skilled precision of a connoisseur.

Her mouth opened to provide a vent for her quickened breathing. To say that she liked what he was doing would have been an understatement. Her heartbeat was racing, and soon it became almost impossible to stop her hips from moving. She was wildly conscious of her body, and the heat and moisture gathering between her thighs. She arched up to him, aching unbearably for something more intense, while tiny involuntary cries fell from her lips. When he put his hand on the most sensitive part of her entire body she froze, but for once he ignored that fact. Through the barrier of her bikini pants he rubbed the tiny hidden bud at the heart of her, and she jerked in surprise before she began to squirm in delight.

He lifted his head to stare down at her, and told her simply and frankly what he wanted to do next. She went even pinker than she was already was, her eyes shifting from his, shock and sudden forbidden longing tearing her in two. Did he really want to…? Could he really want to do *that*? She recalled the intimacy she had already shared with him, and suddenly she was reaching down to help him skim off that last garment.

'Just close your eyes, lie back and enjoy,' Valente urged her thickly, parting her slender thighs.

She was trembling like a leaf, and he willed her to push another boundary back and trust him. He shimmied down the bed, pausing to dip his tongue into the shallow indentation of her tummy button. She giggled, and he tipped her back so that she lay open and naked before him.

Caroline was in shock at what she was allowing, breathing in little shallow pants, her aroused body quivering with an eagerness she could not suppress.

'Stop thinking and shut your eyes,' Valente commanded, settling confidently into the challenge of giving her more pleasure than she had ever dreamt he might give her.

Her sensitised nipples were wet and throbbing, but the heat between her legs was a torment. He teased her with the gentle caress of his fingers when, for the first time in her life, she wanted more force. But he toyed, he tugged, he licked and he suckled at her most private and tender flesh, until sensation consumed her in waves of frantic, writhing, exquisite pleasure. She heard herself whimper and cry out and she really couldn't help it. She was out of control, out of her head at the surging flow of sensation which drove her hunger ever higher, and higher again—higher than she thought she could go. And then suddenly the fierce tension broke, and she reached a climax that rocked her world and made her scream before it splintered through her body like dynamite. After-quakes of sweet shocking pleasure came in ravishing ripples after that, and she lay there splayed like a beached starfish on the bed, in total shock at what had happened to her.

'I never knew…I never dreamt that that's what it would be like,' she whispered dizzily.

'You don't know enough about your body, *belleza mia*.' Valente laughed and pulled her into his arms. 'It's full of wonderful possibilities, and I shall enjoy teaching you about each and every one of them.'

The instant he drew her close she felt the strength of his erection. 'My goodness, I've been so selfish,' she muttered.

'This…here…now…was all about you. I'll take a cold shower. We'll christen our bed in Venice tonight,' Valente announced.

'I'm going to Venice too?' she gasped. 'Tonight?'

'*Si,* I have too much work to do to remain here, and why shouldn't you join me? You can just as easily fly back to the UK from there tomorrow.'

'It's a great idea,'Caroline pronounced with a smile, relieved that he was no longer happy to leave her behind.

Heartbreakingly handsome, his black hair riotously curly after its lengthy assault by her clutching fingers, and with a shadow of stubble roughening his jawline, Valente dealt her a mocking glance. 'I thought so too. You will love Venice.'

Her chin tilted. 'When are you planning to tell me about your past? You still haven't explained how you went from a tiny rented apartment to living like a prince,' she reminded him ruefully.

Valente frowned. 'It's not a pleasant story,' he warned her. 'My mother was a maid in a house owned by Count Ettore Barbieri. My father, Salvatore, was Ettore's eldest son. He was a drunk and a waster. When my mother was seventeen, Salvatore pushed her down on a bed and raped her. I'm the result...'

Caroline stared at him with wide, horrified eyes.

Lean, strong face grim, Valente continued. 'The housekeeper refused to believe my mother and she was dismissed. She went home to her family in Florence, but when they realised she was pregnant they threw her out. They didn't believe her story either. She spent all the years of her youth and my childhood cleaning for a living in Venice. She didn't tell me what had happened to her until I was eighteen, and by then she had cancer.'

Caroline's heart twisted with sympathy, and she gripped his arm to say warmly, 'Valente, I'm so sorry. You must have been devastated.'

'I confronted my father outside one of the clubs he patronised, but he called my mother a whore and his friends beat me up. Salvatore threatened to take my mother to court for spreading lies about him. She was dying,' Valente breathed in disgust. 'But the Barbieri family were well–respected, and when rumours of my mother's accusation spread I suffered a lot of abuse in different quarters. A few years afterwards Salvatore died in a car crash and the Count, my grandfather, asked me to participate in some very discreet DNA testing. For his own peace of mind he wanted to be sure that I wasn't a Barbieri.'

'You must have hated your father's family so much!' Caroline said feelingly.

'I felt sorry for the old man. When my claim was proved, he offered me an allowance to keep quiet and I told him to keep his money. That made him respect me. I refused to be a leech, like the rest of his family. I was studying for a business degree part-time by then, and the

Count promised me my first job when I graduated. But I am very independent and I had my own plans.'

'Knowing you as I do, I expect you did.' Understanding his fierce pride and tough individuality so much better now that he had told her about his divided background and essential aloneness, Caroline snuggled close to him in a silent offering of support and comfort.

'I made my first million on my own. I'm a shark in business, and very good at spotting opportunities,' Valente murmured, with the wolfish assurance that characterised his business approach.

Caroline was buoyant with happiness, relief, and a huge sense of achievement at the success of their growing sexual intimacy. Convinced that she would soon manage to cross the final boundary and consummate their marriage, she was engulfed in a surging flood of love and gratitude. 'Good in bed as well,' she whispered teasingly, wrapping both arms round him and kissing him. 'I love you so much, Valente Lorenzatto!'

In the circle of her clinging arms, his lean, powerful body went rigid. Her declaration of love had felt so natural to her that it took her a moment or two to register that it had had a quite different effect on him. The silence that had fallen was heavy, nerve-racking. Slowly she lifted her pale blonde head to look up at his lean dark face. 'I'm not expecting you to reciprocate,' she told him awkwardly.

'I have no intention of reciprocating,' Valente retorted with sardonic bite, shifting his bronzed shoulders to break her hold and ease back from her. His beautiful dark eyes were hard and unyielding. 'I could never feel that way about you again.'

Shaken by that very extensive rejection, Caroline murmured, 'I shouldn't have said anything. I've got too used to not having to watch my words with you—but you're right. It's far too soon for me to be saying stuff like that.'

'There could never be a right time. I need a shower.' His lean, strong face was cold and set. Springing out of bed, Valente strode into the bedroom next door to use his own bathroom.

I could never feel that way about you again. Why on earth hadn't she kept her mouth shut? How could she have been so foolish as to blurt it out like an infatuated teenager? He still hadn't forgiven her for past events, and by the sound of it he would never do so, she conceded painfully. She cringed for herself, while at the same time fighting off a deep sense of hurt and rejection.

In the shower, she felt those feelings begin to recede, and anger took their place. Valente was full of contradictions and *so* volatile! For almost a month he had played the role of the perfect honeymoon partner and then, without any warning at all, he had turned on her! Everything a considerate lover could do he had done for her. And in bed he had been tender and patient, never putting pressure on her, always letting her set the pace. Was it any wonder that following that long, impossibly slow and very sexy seduction she had told him she loved him? But she had a right to know exactly where she stood with him. She pulled on a light green summer dress and went downstairs.

Koko was still waiting in the hall, and padded in her wake after being petted. Valente was watching the business news in the room he used as an office. He flicked the remote to mute the sound and dealt her a measuring glance. 'I'm not in the mood for an emotional scene, Caroline.'

'As you once said to me,' she framed dulcetly, '*tough*! I need to know where I stand with you.'

'You have a forty–five-page-long pre-nup

that leaves no stone unturned on that score,' Valente reminded her with sardonic cool.

'I thought we'd moved on a little from that,' she admitted tightly, hit on her weakest flank by that reminder of the bricks-and-mortar legal foundation of their far from normal marriage.

'What made you think that? Nothing's changed aside of the fact that we're starting to have some fun in bed. Everything is as it should be.' Brilliant dark eyes rested levelly on her, bright and cold as winter frost. 'As you are very well aware, there is nothing sentimental about our agreement, so talk of love is ridiculous. I've kept my side of the bargain financially, and now I expect you to do what I have paid you to do.'

He had torn the deceptive veil of normality from their relationship and ripped it into tiny shreds, forcing her to face reality—indeed, rubbing her nose in the truth that all he wanted was her body and eventually a child. Her back remained poker-straight, her eyes undimmed. 'No problem. But don't forget that what you sow, you will reap.'

A satiric ebony brow lifted. 'Meaning?' he said, very drily.

'That I'll get over you. Of course I will— because I don't see in you the man I used to

love, and I'm no masochist,' she told him, with
unshaken dignity and her head held high in spite
of the drum of pain starting to beat behind her
left eye—the infallible warning of a migraine
headache. 'But think twice before you ask me
to have a child with you. Does any child deserve
to be raised in the corrosive, bitter atmosphere
of a bad marriage?'

CHAPTER NINE

THE marital bed that lay in the lofty grandeur of the Palazzo Barbieri was not christened that night. Indeed, Valente and Caroline slept in separate bedrooms below the same roof for the first time since they were married.

Caroline's migraine had settled in with a vengeance by the time they boarded the jet. Her medication had barely taken the edge off the drumming pain in her temples, and she'd been nauseous and wretched during the flight. Valente's efforts to provide comfort had rolled off her like water off a duck's back. He was the guy who didn't love her, and just then she hated him.

There hadn't been an ounce of forgiveness in her body during that taxing journey. The housekeeper, Maria, had helped her to get into bed when they'd finally arrived at the vast building on the Grand Canal, the mechanics of having to get there across all that water having merely

exacerbated her misery. She'd lain there in the
shaded room, the pain blinding every other
sense, until a softly spoken doctor had arrived
in Valente's unusually unobtrusive company.
The doctor had given her an injection that had
sent her to sleep, and the last thing she'd
recalled was the comforting feel of Koko's soft
trusting furry warmth nestled against her, and
the realisation that her pet had finally triumphed
over the bedroom ban.

By the following morning Caroline was fine
again. Maria informed her that Valente had
embarked on his day's work in the offices on the
floor below at seven, and Caroline breakfasted
solitarily on a big stone balcony overlooking the
world's most famous waterway.

Early on a bright new day, that glorious,
vibrant, unforgettable view of the city stole her
heart. The magnificent buildings set against an
azure-blue sky and lapped by the canal were
rescued from picture-perfect beauty and
brought to vivid life by the busy surge of water
traffic and the milling crowds in the *campo* on
the opposite bank.

Valente strolled out to join her, Maria
bobbing in his wake to pour him coffee.
Caroline snatched in a slow steadying breath.

As always he looked amazing, sleek and dark and breathtakingly beautiful in a dove-grey designer suit, cut to a perfect fit for his strong, muscular body.

Cradling a cup of black coffee in one hand, he leant back against the ancient stone balustrade, trained liquid dark eyes on her and murmured lazily, 'Feeling better?'

'Back to normal, thankfully.' Even as she looked at him, Caroline was disturbed by an ill-timed recollection of the mind-boggling pleasure he had given her the afternoon before. A dulled ache stirred between her thighs and she shifted uneasily in her seat, her face colouring as agonising awareness washed over her.

'If you want me to, I will come to England with you, *gattina mia,*' Valente informed her smoothly.

Caroline shifted her attention from him to the elegant china on the marble-topped table. Was he taking pity on his pathetic lovelorn wife, who could hardly be looking forward to doing without his divine presence for a few days, or was he just basking in the ego-boosting knowledge that he was adored? Her teeth gritted. She could still barely credit her stupidity in gushing out her love and inviting such humiliation.

'I'll be so taken up with Mum and Dad that

it would be a waste of your time,' she declared briskly.

An attractive brunette PA in a business suit put in a contrite appearance, holding a phone. With an apology Valente took the call, spoke at speed in Italian too fast for Caroline to follow, and tossed the phone down on the table.

'Do you like the view?' he enquired teasingly, evidently untouched by her assurance that his presence was not required in England.

'Yes. Now I know why you once told me that you could never live anywhere else in the world but Venice. All this—' Caroline raised small expressive hands, her appreciation sincere '—would be impossible to match.'

Just as *she* was without match, Valente conceded reluctantly, watching the sunshine gleam over the silvery pale long hair pooling in silken loops over her slight shoulders and then highlight her flawless skin, sparkling eyes and soft pink mouth. Seeing her in his home felt surreal. But such thoughts spooked him, since he was a very practical man. Somewhere— possibly even within the beloved city of his birth, he assured himself—there might well be another woman equally beautiful and possessed of Caroline's special appeal. That imaginary woman might even be less complex than the woman he had married, and a great deal more entertaining, he told himself in emphatic addition. No woman was irreplaceable or irresistible. Nor had any woman ever been necessary to his comfort and peace of mind. He didn't need Caroline; no matter how hard she tried to entangle him in her sentimental promises she would fail—because he would never allow a woman to have that much power over him again.

Yet, in spite of those reassuringly cautious reflections, Valente could not stop studying his wife's attractions, nor seeking to pinpoint the source of them. She did that looking-up-through–the-eyelashes thing that all women did to flirt, yet in spite of her essential innocence there was a curiously sultry gleam of promise in her misty grey gaze that made the fit of Valente's well-cut trousers uncomfortably tight. He regarded her broodingly from below luxuriant lashes, resenting the fate that would remove her from his bed when he most wanted her there, despising the ache at his groin. It would do him good to cool off without her for a few days.

Her body was already reacting without her

volition to the growing heat of Valente's appraisal. Her nipples were pushing against her green lace bra, her breasts felt constricted in the cups, and her heart was racing. And, angry though she still was with him, she could neither stifle that physical tumult of response nor break the hot connection with his gaze.

Valente reached a sudden decision. There would be plenty of time for him to cool off while she was in England with her family! She was his wife. He didn't need to practice self-denial now. Who was he trying to impress? He swept up the phone to cancel all his appointments, unmoved by his senior PA's astonishment at his instruction because business always came first with Valente. But if there had ever been a good excuse for breaking the rules it was Caroline, sitting there, huge pearl-grey eyes pinned to him, a silk top lovingly moulded to her delicate curves, a short floral skirt revealing her long slender legs.

He extended a lean long-fingered hand to her. 'Come here…'

His charisma proved stronger than her antagonism or her wariness. Quivering with tension, she took his hand and he pulled her close. She buried her head in his shoulder and drank in the gloriously familiar scent of him before she let him walk her back into the *palazzo*—through the grand drawing room, with its superb Murano glass chandeliers adorned with flowers and cupids, and up the stairs to the remarkable master bedroom suite, with its hand-painted murals of frolicking gods and goddesses.

'Take off your jacket,' she told him, standing dead centre of the room.

Amusement gave a dazzling edge to his handsome smile. The jacket was cast aside with a flourish. Caroline undid his tie and began unbuttoning his shirt. Although she was absolutely determined to be a full partner, her hands were a little shaky, and he yanked his shirt out in the same moment that he bent his arrogant dark head and kissed her, long and hard and hungrily, one hand meshed in her hair to hold her still and deepen the penetration of her tongue. Liquid lightning travelled through her, firing up every skin cell with anticipation.

With a hungry groan and a dangerous light in his scorching golden eyes, Valente freed her and stepped back from her. 'I'm sorry, I must be scaring you, *gattina mia*. I'm too fired up to be gentle. Perhaps this is not a good idea.'

Caroline stretched her taut shoulders before moving forward, confidence fizzing through her veins like a shot of adrenalin. She wanted to be the same as every other woman. She didn't want him to hold back and handle her with kid gloves, as if she was precious glass he might crack. She didn't want him to protect her from his passion. He had already taught her that all cats were not grey in the dark. She had gone way beyond the stage of expecting Valente to hurt her or scare her, as Matthew had once done.

'I'm not scared any more,' she whispered urgently. 'I liked that kiss. I like the feeling that you're on the edge…'

His burning gaze made her blush, and he urged her back to him with impatient hands, covering her ripe mouth with his while he backed her down on the bed. 'I'm always on the edge with you,' he admitted roughly. 'But if you're still *virgo intacta*, I can't promise that this won't hurt a little. I don't know. You're my first virgin.'

Caroline wanted to be his one and only, his last. But desire and the need to experience what other women took for granted had a headier hold on Caroline than the emotions that had brought her hurt and humiliation only the day before. Her body still humming from the erotic mastery of that kiss, she whispered tautly, 'I want you, and I don't want to wait any longer.'

It was all the encouragement that Valente needed. Between kisses he extracted her from her fine silk top, pausing to admire the rigid pink buds already poking through the lace of her bra. His hunger at a tormenting high, he bent her back and suckled those ripe buds through the delicate lace, shifting between one and the other while she gasped and jerked. He pushed up her skirt, parted her thighs, scored his finger down over the taut seam of fabric and felt the dampness there with an earthy groan of satisfaction.

'I used to dream of having you dressed up in the most expensive lingerie,' he confided with dark amusement as he released the fastener on her bra. 'But now I've got you in it, I just want to rip it off you again.'

He stripped her naked with very little regard for the longevity of the items, but she didn't care because he was kissing her in hungry, breathless bursts that made her tingle all over. He addressed his attention to her rose-tipped breasts, sucking on the distended tips until she was almost unbearably aroused. And then, when she thought she could take no more, when she was crying out to be touched, he traced the tender damp folds of her womanhood and parted them to discover her narrow channel. His thumb rubbed the swollen pouting bud below her mound, and from that moment on she was writhing and drowning in sensation so intense it was an exquisite torment.

By the time Valente rolled her under him she was so excited that her every skin cell yearned for the next step. He pushed a pillow under her hips to raise her. 'You're very small, and I'm shockingly excited, *tesoro mia.*'

She was more than ready for the hard, hot probe of his separating the tight wet walls of her most tender flesh. Instinct made her arch back and his passage eased. He sank into her in a long, deep surge of power, and there was a sharp flash of pain which made her tense up and bite her lip. But even that didn't stop her glorying in the strong feel of him inside her, didn't stop her tightening her inner muscles and watching his beautiful dark golden eyes semi-close with sexual pleasure.

'Okay?' he prompted anxiously.

'Better than,' she told him shakily. 'I like it.'

'I hope so,' Valente traded with an erotic

smile. 'I have high hopes of persuading you to repeat this pleasure over and over again.'

And, while she was more than satisfied at the wondrous intimacy of his possession, she was thoroughly stunned by the delight of what happened to her when he began to glide in and out of her eager body. Excitement blazed a trail through her and she clung, surrendering to the hot, drugging pleasure of his every thrust. She cried out at the passionate peak of the orgasm which sent her shooting to the stars.

'I want to pack you in my suitcase to take back to England,' Caroline confessed dizzily.

Valente laughed out loud and leant over her to kiss her, smoothing her tumbled hair off her damp brow. 'I hope that was a compliment, because I found you amazing, *belleza mia*.'

With every fibre of her being she wanted to hug him and kiss him and express her emotions, but she rigorously suppressed those promptings because they could only embarrass her. There was going to be no more of that nonsense! No more emotional outpourings calculated to stroke his ego!

'You were amazing too—but then that's only to be expected with all the experience you've had,' Caroline replied carelessly. 'At least I don't need to be afraid of sex any more, and we can have as much fun in bed as you like. After all, it has to be the only thing we have in common.'

Valente was not quite sure how to take that assurance, but he didn't like the tone of it. 'We are married,' he reminded her seriously.

'Sexually speaking,' Caroline added. 'How long will it be before you get bored with me?'

Valente sat up and sent her a flashing glance of censure. 'I'm not going to get bored with you. You're my wife!'

'Does that mean you're going to be the only lover I ever have?' Caroline enquired, in a forlorn tone of disappointment.

'Yes, it bloody well does!' Valente raked back explosively, and thrust back the bedding to get up. 'What's got into you?'

A ferocious desire to wind him up, she might have admitted, had she been in a sympathetic mood—but she wasn't. 'You're the one who told me not to bring sentiment into our marriage.'

'There's a fine line between candour and bad taste,' he spelt out coolly.

'Would it be bad taste for me to ask who the turquoise wrap at the Villa belonged to?'

His bold bronzed profile tensed. '*Si*, and inappropriate.'

'Well, I thought it was tacky that the evidence of her occupation wasn't removed before I arrived,' Caroline traded.

'Point taken,' Valente breathed with sardonic bite. 'May we now close the subject?'

Caroline slid out of bed. 'I have packing to do.'

'Your maid can take care of that—I need you to take care of me,' Valente murmured huskily.

Caroline, already conscious of the slight ache of discomfort at the heart of her, thought that a repeat bout of lovemaking would be unwise. With a rueful smile she vanished into the bathroom, reflecting that Valente, with his high-voltage energy and powerful libido, would take a good deal of taking care of in the sex department, so it was hardly a source of surprise that women like the turquoise wrap lady featured in his life. Whether it was reasonable or otherwise, Caroline could not help wishing that he had never had a need for other women. She also hoped that, unlike Matthew, Valente did not suffer from an ongoing desire for sexual variety and fresh conquests to satisfy his ego. She was in a marriage where she could afford to take nothing for granted.

She used the rest of the day, with the help of the staff, to set up her workshop in an allocated room at the back of the house. She sorted out her stock, and checked her mail for the first time in a couple of weeks. The little ornamental cats she had once collected sparkled in their gorgeous jewel colours on the windowsill, and she began to wonder how she could design a new line of jewellery with Murano glass. It took her a couple of hours to package the orders from her website and organise their dispatch. It was a wrench to leave the workshop without making anything, for she loved the creative thrill of designing a new piece, but by then it was time for her to get changed for her flight.

Shortly before her departure, Valente discovered her in her workshop. He smiled at the cat ornaments, most of which he had given her, and lingered to take a keen look at the jewellery. He was very impressed, recognising the artistry and design in the well-crafted pieces. With a frown he switched off his mobile phone when it began its insistent ring.

'You're always so busy,' she murmured tautly, tense at the prospect of leaving him, but thinking that with the long work hours he maintained she would hardly be missed.

'I took almost a month off to be with you in Tuscany,' he reminded her, framing her cheekbones with long graceful fingers, locking her in stasis by the simple act of focusing his brilliant dark eyes on her. 'During that time I delegated, and blunders were made. This is payback time, *belezza mia*.'

Her eyes slid shut as he captured her mouth in an intoxicating kiss and suckled her swollen lips with devouring sensuality. Heat curled through her defenceless body, rousing a languorous throb of response in tender places. She couldn't breathe for longing as he dipped his tongue in a moist sweep of her tender mouth.

'Enough,' Valente growled thickly, easing out onto the landing outside the room. Splaying a hand to her spine, he directed her down the magnificent staircase which gave access to his offices from the ground floor.

Her slender body all of a quiver, after that bone-melting kiss that had encouraged her to cling rather than walk away, Caroline negotiated the stairs slowly, for her legs felt as if they didn't quite belong to the rest of her. There was a woman at the foot of the stairs—a gorgeous redhead with a luscious leggy figure revealed rather than concealed by the neat fit of the white linen dress she wore.

His lean, powerful frame tensing against

Caroline's, Valente turned to say something to his wife as they stepped down into the outrageously grand foyer. Before he could speak, however, the woman neatly stepped between the two of them. Kissing Valente on both cheeks, she addressed him in a flood of Italian before finally sparing a rather mocking glance in Caroline's direction. 'I'm Agnese Brunetti, an old friend of Valente's. *Dios mio*! You are really tiny! Do you speak Italian?'

'I'm afraid not.'

'Of course Valente and I both speak to each other in Veneziano, the local dialect,' Agnese shared, shooting Valente a rueful chummy smile. 'We're members of a very exclusive club. Every year there are fewer and fewer of us able to converse in the old way.'

Caroline was chilled to find herself looking up at the statuesque redhead. Matthew had betrayed her with other women too often for her to be anything other than suspicious of such a bold beauty. She knew instantly, in that strange way a woman could, that she was meeting the owner of the flamboyant silk robe left behind at the Tuscan villa. Still inconsequentially chattering in a mixture of what Caroline could only assume was Veneziano and English, Agnese touched Valente's sleeve once and his lapel in a second, more lingering demonstration of physical ease, making no attempt to conceal her familiarity with him. On hyper-alert, Caroline picked up on the other woman's every move and change of expression.

'I'm sorry, but Caroline has a flight to catch,' Valente breathed coolly, extracting them at speed from the encounter. He signalled one of his hovering staff and asked him to take Agnese Brunetti up to his office. 'I'll be with you shortly,' he told her.

'I've known Agnese for a long time,' he added casually as he helped Caroline into the waiting motor launch tied up at the splendid front doors of the *palazzo*.

In a horizontal manner of speaking, Caroline affixed with an inner shudder of recoil. Agnese was his mistress. Past or present? All the way to the airport Caroline tormented herself with unwise comparisons. The beautiful redhead's voluptuous curves had reminded her of Matthew's preferences and made her feel inadequate. Suddenly it was a relief to be travelling back to England, to escape the pressure of her marriage and the humiliation of unrequited love and concentrate instead on her father's health and her mother's worries on the same issue.

Joe and Isabel Hales were still staying in a hotel, and Winterwood was in control of the builders, as work on both house and apartment proceeded at a rapid pace.

Having first inspected the impressive renovations taking place at Winterwood, Caroline checked into the same hotel as her parents and accompanied them to the hospital for her father's admittance. Isabel was beside herself with concern that her husband might die on the operating table, and she needed her daughter to keep her calm.

Joe was in surgery for three hours, but the operation was pronounced a success. And, although her father was weak afterwards, within a few days Caroline could see his strength beginning to return. Valente had already had the brochures of several luxurious convalescent homes sent to Isabel, so that she could choose where she and her husband would stay after Joe was released from hospital. Once that move was made, Caroline began to feel rather superfluous to requirements.

Valente phoned her every day. She wanted

to ask about Agnese, but was determined not to sound like some clingy, over-possessive wife, suspicious of every woman who came near her husband.

And yet, in truth, Caroline reckoned that she *was*. In a loveless marriage it was a challenge for Caroline to believe that one woman could be enough for Valente.

At the end of the second week, Valente flew over from Italy to visit her parents. When he arrived at the convalescent home he had two of his business team in tow, for he had had a couple of business calls to make locally. Joe was asking her husband eager questions about the future for Hales Transport when Caroline arrived and found him there. It amazed her to see how relaxed her parents had become with him. It was hard to believe that just five years earlier they had behaved as though he was Public Enemy Number One. But his generosity towards them, and his care during a time of crisis, had reassured the older couple and given him the status of a trusted family member.

'So, what are you planning to do about our competitor, Bomark Logistics?' Joe was asking eagerly when his daughter arrived.

'I think there's room for both businesses in

the current market,' Valente responded with care, glancing up to see Caroline in the doorway of the large conservatory where the patients entertained their visitors.

With her pale blonde hair casually pulled back from her lovely face, and wearing a dress the colour of lavender teamed with a short-sleeved cashmere cardigan, she exuded the fresh, natural appeal of a wild flower—and she still took her highly sophisticated husband's breath away. As arousal stabbed into him like a particularly vicious knife he went rigid, and mentally regrouped from that over-the-top reaction to his first sight of her in thirteen days. She was incredibly pretty—but so were thousands of other women, he instructed himself grimly. He could not, however, prevent his wayward thoughts from reaching a peak of proud satisfaction over the knowledge that she was his wife, and therefore exclusively his. She had let him down badly once, and he would never give her the chance to do that again. But, flawed or otherwise, he was willing to admit that she was the one acquisition he was most proud of.

Caroline said her goodbyes to her parents before her return to Italy with Valente. While she talked to them she stole little glances at her husband, for she had missed his charismatic, unsettling presence more than she would ever have admitted during her visit to her former home. He was far too good-looking and sexually compelling for her peace of mind. All too many nights since they had parted she had lain awake, wondering if he was awake too, if he was experiencing anything like the acute pain of separation that was tormenting her. She had worried that the gorgeous Agnese and all her predatory equivalents would be hovering around Valente, all too keen to offer him sexual consolation. She had feared that he might be tempted. He shot her a brief sidewise glance from dense dark-lashed eyes the colour of caramel toffee and she felt almost sick with longing, her mouth going dry, her heartbeat picking up speed.

'It's hard to believe that my parents think the sun rises and sets on you now, but it does make life much more simple,' Caroline allowed, shaking her head over the meteoric leap in status he had contrived in the senior Haleses' eyes as she and Valente followed his aides out of the visiting area.

'But I should have been here with you when

Joe had his op,' Valente breathed in a tone of regret. 'That was wrong.'

'My parents know how busy you are, and you've been so generous in spite of old history,' she said gratefully.

'But business should never come before family. Ettore told me that once, and I should have listened harder. He was so busy making money in order to live like his forebears had lived that his children were like strangers to him. He gave them money and little else, and of course they took advantage. By the time I got to know him his descendants were picking his old bones as clean as a pack of vultures. They all enjoyed riding the gravy train at his expense,' Valente revealed with a grimace. 'That was why I agreed to try and steer the Barbieri family fortunes into more profitable waters.'

'You cared about your grandfather. I'm glad you had that bond with him,' Caroline said warmly.

Valente winced. 'He was an honourable man, and was once a shrewd businessman in his own right, but by the time I met him he was going blind and was dangerously dependent on his family. He needed my help because he had learned that he couldn't trust them any more.'

'You didn't seem very close to the cousins who came to our wedding,' Caroline commented.

'I'm not. I restored my grandfather's fortunes, and he changed his will and left his property empire to me instead. You can imagine how popular that made me.'

'You had rights too, as the son of your grandfather's eldest child,' Caroline argued.

'The title of count, of course, went to my cousin, as he was born within marriage, unlike me, but he was denied the ancestral homes and the money,' Valente revealed wryly. 'Ettore didn't trust him or his sisters to spend what needed to be spent on repairing the properties, and I must admit that I have spent a great deal more conserving them than I originally intended.'

'How do your relatives live now?'

'I set some of them up in business, and I employ another few and help out some of the older relations with an allowance. We don't socialise much. In their eyes, I'll always be the boy from the backstreet *calle* who shamed the family by exposing my father's crime. Only Ettore was able to accept me as I am.'

As they crossed the gravel to the waiting limousine his aides were exchanging files. A gust of wind made one of the files flap open and caught a sheet of paper, which fluttered up into the air and fell down at Caroline's feet. She stooped to pick it up and the name of the business and the familiar logo printed across the top startled her and made her stare: Bomark Logistics. It was some kind of a report. She passed it back to Valente's aide without comment and wondered what dealings he had with the rival transport firm which had put Hales out of business. Was he trying to buy it? Take it over? Or was he checking out the opposition by some nefarious means?

That gave her two topics she wanted to discuss with him in some detail: Agnese Brunetti and Bomark logistics. Valente had a dark, secretive Venetian soul, and he fiercely conserved his privacy. She took a deep breath when she got into the limousine and turned to him, but by then he was already on the phone. It would be easier to tackle those topics on the flight back to Italy, she decided ruefully.

But Valente had other more pressing plans…

CHAPTER TEN

DARK eyes flashing hot gold, Valente caught Caroline in his arms within minutes of the jet taking off. 'I missed you, *bella mia*.'

Her heart raced while she tossed her head in apparent surprise and her grey eyes sparkled with challenge. 'You never mentioned it when you phoned. Not once.'

Valente threw his handsome dark head back, laughed in appreciation and shrugged a broad shoulder with magnificent disregard for such frills. 'So, I'm not one of those guys who will say all the right things to feed your ego!'

Pained regret stirred inside her. 'But you used to be much more…emotional, open and affectionate.'

His amusement evaporated. 'Women like you toughened me up. Don't complain about your own handiwork,' he breathed harshly, bending his proud dark head to nuzzle the tender skin of her pale slender throat with his lips and the edge of his strong white teeth in an unexpectedly erotic salutation that made her nerve-endings execute a somersault.

'You're not being fair.' Caroline was annoyed, tired of being censured for what had happened five years earlier. He had also made choices with far-reaching consequences, when he had left the country and made it impossible for her to contact him other than by letter.

'Since when was life fair?' In an effort to conclude the conversation, Valente kissed her with all the seething passion that had built up during her absence. He had not slept a night through since her departure.

Caroline's hostility took a back seat while she trembled in convulsive response against his lean, powerful frame. His hands splayed to her small bottom to lift her and gather her closer, making her awesomely aware of the virile heat of his erection. 'I want you so much I ache,' Valente groaned.

And there would be no real conversation until after that stage, she recognised ruefully, and then just as quickly scolded herself for that thought. Only weeks ago he would not have dared to show her that passion, and she would have cringed away from him, still too damaged by her experiences with Matthew to have any prospect of rediscovering or enjoying her own sexuality.

Headily conscious of the power Valente had given back to her, and convinced that no man who had been 'playing away' behind her back could possibly be so hot for her, Caroline found herself gurgling with appreciative laughter when he virtually dragged her into the sleeping compartment. Never had she felt so desirable, and yet at that moment, as they sought out the only privacy available to them, she felt more like a teenager than a grown-up. She was a willing partner when they shed their clothes in a heap and somehow synchronised into a heated, twisting, yearning tumble of bodies on the bed in urgent pursuit of the same elemental satisfaction. The excitement he generated with his first driving thrust never dropped for so much as a second of their fevered lovemaking. When her release came it was explosive, and Valente stifled her noisy cries with his mouth and a deep sense of sweetness possessed her heart.

Drifting back from that ecstatic reunion of the senses, Caroline never wanted to move again, and marvelled that she had contrived to live without Valente for two weeks. She was finding an extraordinary peace in lying within the circle of his arms, for he was so rarely still and quiet. She could rejoice covertly in the wonderful smell of his damp bronzed skin and the glorious intimacy of being with him again when, five years ago, she had truly believed that hope and joy were gone for ever. And if it was different now, because he didn't want her love, was *anything* perfect? Was she planning to give up what they had for a life in which she would be bereft without him? In that moment, she thought not.

'We'll be landing in less than an hour, *belezza mia*. We need to move.' Valente shifted away from her with a sigh that she wanted to believe signified disappointment at that restricted time-frame.

Before he could leave her side, however, Caroline was determined to satisfy her curiosity on certain issues. 'There are a couple of things I want to ask you about.'

'Agnese?' Valente guessed with alarming accuracy, turning his tousled curly dark head to shoot her an infuriatingly knowing glance. 'Yes, we were lovers—and now it's over because I have you.'

'So why was she coming to see you?'

'She was hoping that a month of marriage

would have changed my mind and that I would be ready to take her back. Agnese doesn't lack self-belief.'

'Oh…' His candour surprised her, for put under pressure Matthew had lied and lied and lied again, so that it had become hard for her to accept anything at face value. 'Were you in love with her?'

'It was more a convenient arrangement than a love affair.'

'You're saying that she was your mistress?'

'Yes, I paid her bills, and she… Surely you don't need me to explain any more?'

Involuntarily, Carole was shocked. 'But it sounds so cold-blooded!'

'It suited us both. Not everyone wants emotional ties and promises, Caroline,' he imparted with sardonic cool.

'I have just one more question,' Caroline continued, half under her breath, studiously ignoring that wounding gibe. 'What's your involvement with Bomark Logistics back home?'

Valente went as still as a man who had been told a ticking time bomb was attached to him. 'We'll talk about that in depth when we get home,' he responded with measured cool.

Caroline was bewildered by that response.

In depth? What was he suggesting? Of the two issues, she had ironically considered the topic of Agnese Brunetti the more controversial and the least likely to lead to a satisfactory conclusion. She had even thought he might refuse to satisfy her inquisitiveness. After all, his relationship with Agnese before their marriage was really none of her business. The question about Bomark Logistics had only been asked out of casual curiosity. Why was he holding back on giving her an immediate explanation?

As they completed their trip back to the Palazzo Barbieri, Caroline became increasingly disturbed by Valente's preoccupation. The tight lines of his bold profile and the grim set of his mouth made her tense, and uneasy as well. It was an anti-climax when Koko darted out of the shadows in the entrance hall and leapt at Caroline in welcome, only to struggle to be set down again so that she could enact the same welcome for Valente as well.

'How on earth did you manage to persuade her into liking you?' Caroline exclaimed, astounded to see her formerly hostile pet now winding round Valente's trouser legs with a purr as loud as a steam engine.

'You were gone. I had no competition. She

was lonely,' Valente pointed out, lifting the little Siamese and stroking her in reward for her enthusiastic greeting.

In the glorious drawing room, with the crimson light of the dying sun filtering in through the balcony doors across the muted antique colours of the beautiful Persian rug, he finally faced her. 'How did you find out that I had a connection with Bomark Logistics?'

Caroline explained, and it transpired that Valente had not even noticed the tiny incident in which she had picked up the revealing document when the wind dropped it at her feet.

'So, you don't know anything,' Valente pronounced, his ebony brows drawing together, the angles of his lean hard features saturnine in the dusk light. 'I could lie. And I am tempted to lie, because I know you won't like the truth. But in terms of business I did nothing wrong. It's a dog-eat-dog world out there.'

'What on earth are you talking about?' Caroline pressed in growing bewilderment. 'Have you bought out Bomark Logistics, or something? Did you think I would be annoyed at that because the firm put Hales out of business? I'm not that foolish…'

Valente surveyed her levelly. 'I set up Bomark

from scratch three years ago. I own it, and I am responsible for every move the firm has made since then.'

The blankness of shock had wiped all expression from Caroline's face. 'But that's not possible. You own it? Have always owned it? I mean why…three years ago?'

'I opened another haulage business in order to compete with Hales and had your manager, Sweetman, head-hunted into a London position,' Valente clarified with reluctance.

'But why?' Caroline demanded again. 'You actually *wanted* to put my family out of business?'

Valente nodded confirmation in silence. He had not expected her to be quite so shocked. A devious woman would have recognised the strings he had pulled and understood why without asking. Caroline, however, clearly did not comprehend what he was trying to explain.

'I don't understand. I know you must have been very angry and bitter when I didn't turn up to marry you five years ago,' she murmured tightly. 'But why would you go to such appalling lengths to target a small family business?'

'I blamed your family for what happened as much as I blamed you.'

A stricken look crossed Caroline's visage. 'But you *knew* there was no way I could have made it to the church. You *knew* how sorry I was that my message didn't reach you in time,' she reasoned feverishly. 'I know my parents behaved badly, and that you were treated unfairly, but I don't believe that we did anything that could excuse you for deliberately setting out to destroy our business.'

Valente was wondering why she was saying that there had been no way she could have made it to the church. He was exasperated by his ignorance of the excuses she had no doubt employed in that letter, but determined not to expose it. As for this message she was now mentioning for the first time: he did not believe there had ever been one. Her family had wanted rid of him by any means, and ensuring that he was left standing like a fool at the altar had been a very effective method of deterring him from seeking any further contact.

'I wanted you all to pay for what you did,' Valente confessed.

A humourless laugh was wrenched from her soft pink mouth. 'You don't think three and a half years of marriage to Matthew Bailey was penance enough for me?'

Valente wore a guarded look that gave nothing away. 'As far as I knew at the time you were enjoying a happy marriage with your childhood sweetheart. It was only after Bailey's death that I learned that it hadn't been quite that perfect.'

'But Matthew and I were never childhood sweethearts!' Caroline argued with spirit. 'Where did you get that idea? We were friends—casual friends. I thought a lot of him, and I respected his opinion. I admit that I was entirely taken in by him until I became his wife. But there was never any romance between us—either before or after we married. I married him on the rebound.'

'The phrase "childhood sweethearts" came from your own father's lips. Joe came to see me the week before our wedding and accused me of having come between you and Matthew and ruining your life. He said it was Matthew whom you really loved and he tried to buy me off.'

Caroline was aghast. 'Why didn't you tell me that Dad had done that? I had no idea.'

'There had already been enough bad feeling, and you were living on your nerves. I didn't want to put you under any more pressure and I was confident that you loved me,' Valente admitted, with a bitter twist to his handsome mouth.

'I did love you…I *did*!' Caroline proclaimed in a shaken tone. 'But you never responded to my letters. You never phoned. You don't *do* emotion or forgiveness, do you? The very fact it's taken almost two months for us even to discuss the past says it all. You just scrubbed me out of your life like I didn't matter to you!'

His lean strong face was darkening with indignation. 'What did you expect after leaving me standing at the church? It would be a rare man who could forgive an offence of that magnitude.'

'You just didn't love me enough, Valente,' Caroline condemned vehemently. 'When you tell me now that you'll never feel like that for me again, it's not really that great a loss, is it? A man who really loved me would have overcome his injured pride and talked to me again—but not you. So much for love! You just deserted me.'

Lean, olive-skinned features hard with anger, Valente spread wide his arms and threw up both hands in a bold physical demonstration of his wrathful rejection of that scenario. 'I… deserted…*you*?'

'I was crushed. I thought I had nothing left to live for—and there was Matthew, being a very sympathetic and staunch friend in my hour of need,' Caroline recalled, stinging tears filling her eyes as she looked back at that fateful period of her life. 'Before very long my parents were pointing out how happy they would be if I married Matthew. He proposed. You weren't there. I gave in to the pressure—a marriage of friends, Matt called it, but even our friendship didn't last. Yes, I was an idiot, and I let myself fell into a stupid trap, but if I hadn't been so unhappy I would never have been that silly!'

Her explanation bore not the smallest resemblance to Valente's assumptions at the time. 'I thought you had only used me to make Matthew jealous. I also believed that you had realised you loved him more than me.'

With an unsteady hand, Caroline dashed away her tears. 'Well, maybe if you'd had enough interest you would have found out the truth for yourself.' Her grey eyes darkened and her soft mouth compressed. 'But why are we even having this conversation now?'

'We're having it because it's a conversation we should have had a long time ago,' Valente conceded between gritted white teeth, violently wound up by her accusations and full of rage, but refusing to parade the emotions storming through him.

'All that doesn't matter any more. I'm more interested in your ownership of Bomark Logistics,' Caroline admitted, bringing the dialogue full circle back to what she saw as the most important question. 'That you chose, three years after we broke up, to pursue a goal of revenge at any cost truly horrifies me. It proves all over again to me that I must be a rotten judge of character.'

'I'm not like you, *bella mia*,' Valente breathed. 'When someone injures me I don't turn the other cheek, and I never will.'

A belligerent glint in her usually soft gaze, Caroline drew herself up straight to her full height. She was so tense that her muscles ached in protest at her stance. 'But to have set up another haulage firm solely to destroy my family's livelihood is beyond forgiveness.'

'I wanted you. All along, my only goal was to gain access to you.'

'But you started this three years ago, when Matthew was still alive and I was his wife!'

Valente veiled his black-lashed unrepentant gaze. He had pinned his colours to the mast and he wasn't the man to retreat. 'Whether you were married or otherwise made no difference to me.'

Caroline rested shaken eyes on him and then

turned away, wandering over to the windows to stare sightlessly out at the superbly evocative Venetian skyline. He was so aggressive, so destructive, so unashamed of the methods he had employed. In a word? Ruthless. Yet once he had shielded her from that side of his character, persuading her that he was a much more humane and understanding character. *This* was the man she loved?

'No cost was too high to pay, was it?' Caroline accused in a sudden surge of disgust as she totted up the consequences of his behaviour. 'What do you think the slow decline of Hales and the loss of those contracts did to my father's health? It broke his heart. It was his father's firm, and he was horribly ashamed that he couldn't keep it in business. You didn't care that you were hurting my family because you still thought I had let you down.'

His jawline took on an even more stubborn angle. He stood there with the macho air of a male urging her to throw whatever she liked at him and see how well he would withstand the barrage. 'You *did* let me down.'

'How did I let you down? By falling ill? By being in hospital the night before our wedding? How was that my fault?' Caroline launched at him shakily. 'That was fate. The second thoughts and the doubts and fears that tormented me the next morning while you were at the church *were* my fault. I admit that, but I still wasn't well enough to get out of that bed and do anything for myself.'

'I don't know what you're talking about,' Valente was forced to growl, the reference to hospital having cut through his reserve and ignited his frustration. 'I told you that I didn't read your letters.'

'Any…of them?' she prompted unsteadily, before turning away, her hand crammed to her wobbly mouth. Further speech seemed pointless. She had poured out her heart in those letters and all to no avail—for he had not even taken the time to read what she had written.

Pulling herself back together again, Caroline focused on Valente with stark denunciation in her eyes. 'You're not the man I thought you were even five years ago. You're more damaged than I could ever have realised. Although you set out to destroy my family, you forgave the family of the man who raped your mother…I don't understand. Why couldn't you forgive my parents or me?'

Rigid with self-discipline, Valente bit back

the hot words brimming on his lips and watched
her turn on her heel and walk to the door.
'Where are you going?'

'I'm going to lie down…I'm scared I've got
another migraine coming on,' she admitted
grudgingly, rubbing her fingers across the tightness beginning to band round her temples. 'And
then I'm flying back to England as soon as it
can be arranged—because you scare me.'

'How do I scare you?' Valente demanded
angrily, outraged by that indictment.

'You tell me you've been plotting against me
and my family for years and you don't understand why I'm scared of you?' Her voice broke
at the height of that incredulous question. 'Do
you think that's *normal* behaviour?'

Caroline lay on their bed in a stupor of distress
and shock. How could he have been so cruel as
to deliberately destroy her family's livelihood?
All right, her parents were not his parents, but
they were at a vulnerable age. Had he no conscience at all? Of course, how many people had
shown Valente love? No doubt his mother had
loved him, but she had died when he was only
a teenager, and only after gifting him the bitter
knowledge that he was a child born of rape.

Valente had only ever known the rougher, more painful faces of lust and love. He still believed Caroline had let him down deliberately five years earlier. How could any man be so stubborn in holding on to his convictions? Yet now, ironically, she understood him so much better, for his image was now clear in her mind. He had scorned her love in the present because he had no faith in her past claims of love. The love of women like Agnese Brunetti had been for his money, and his lean, powerful body, not for the essential male behind the fine feathers.

And no feathers came more fine, Caroline conceded, studying the opulent grandeur of her surroundings with pained eyes. The child of rape had triumphed in worldly terms, but not before suffering many vicissitudes and rejections. It hurt to appreciate that she only figured as one more rejection in his chequered life, yet she had loved him so much. And whatever he had felt for her had been strong enough, enduring enough, to bring him back to her five years on. In fact, over a long period of time he had put in an enormous amount of effort to ensure that when he did re-enter her life he was in an unbeatable position of power and influence. It would be a bit of a come-down for him if he was ever to realise that all he had really had to do was make himself available, and one or way or another she would have come back to him of her own free will.

Valente leafed impatiently through the contents of his safe in the library. He was in a blind rage, and the feeling of being almost out of control unnerved him. At last he extracted a letter, no longer white and fresh, in a fat, battered envelope. Why had he kept it when he refused to lower himself to the level of reading it? He had dumped all those that came afterwards unread. Well, now he would find out what Caroline had been talking about…doubtless some stupid tangle of lying excuses designed to make him think better of her.

He sat down with a glass of the Villa Barbieri's finest wine and ripped open the envelope with something less than his usual cool. There were eight pages of Caroline's handwriting to be as-similated. He flattened the first sheet to read, and the breathless over-the-top opening made him acknowledge for the first time how young Caroline had still been in those days, 'My dearest, darling, beloved Valente…' it began.

Something twisted inside him, and he began

to read with more appetite than he had had when he first lifted the letter. She claimed to have been rushed into hospital with a burst appendix the night before their wedding. Valente went cold, for he was recalling the small seam of scar tissue on her lower abdomen which he had noticed and intended to ask her about—until the pull of her proximity had driven the seemingly minor matter from his mind. Adrenalin pumping through him, he read on at speed. She had been on the operating table fighting for her life while he had been waiting for her at the church. She had asked her father to ensure that Valente was informed and brought to see her, but Joe Hales had passed on that responsibility to Matthew instead. Matthew had, in turn, refused to leave the hospital until Caroline was out of danger.

Reeling in shock from what he had learned, Valente plunged upright and strode off to find Caroline straight away. He did not know what he was going to say to her. He only knew that it was of the utmost importance that he talked to her, as he had never talked to her in the entirety of their relationship, and that was a challenge he was not even sure he could meet.

He glanced into her workshop before he went

upstairs. The glass cats still sparkled in the light coming through the window. He was touched that she had kept them all these years.

A floorboard creaked in the master bedroom and Caroline's lashes swept up: Valente was stationed at the foot of the bed, rather like the Grim Reaper in a designer suit. 'Have you got a migraine?' he asked.

'No, I think it was just the tension getting to me.'

'I never read that letter you sent me five years ago,' Valente admitted harshly.

'There were at least six of them.'

'I dumped them without reading them—but I kept the first one you sent.'

Her smooth brow indented. 'Why would you keep it and not read it?'

'I was like an addict resisting temptation,' Valente confided, squaring his chin. 'Even as recently as two months ago I was proud of my ability to resist opening that letter. I didn't want to read your excuses for fear that I would mellow towards you, and my pride wouldn't allow me to run that risk.'

Conscious that Valente had to be in a very strange mood to be talking about such promptings, Caroline slowly levered herself up from her prone position. 'You resisted my letter as if it was a dangerous drug?' she rephrased, wondering if she could possibly have heard him right—because she had never dreamt that he might suffer from such quixotic thoughts and reactions.

'I didn't read it until tonight. It was a…a devastating experience,' he confessed in a jerky undertone, his strain pronounced. 'You were sick. I wasn't there when you needed me.'

'Nobody told you I needed you or that I was ill.'

'But I should have considered the possibility.'

'I tried to phone you that evening—'

Valente rested tormented dark eyes full of regret on her. 'I chucked my mobile phone off the bridge into the river beside the church because I didn't want to be tempted into phoning you. I wanted to be strong.'

'Well, you were certainly that,' Caroline conceded. 'Why didn't it occur to you that something had to be badly wrong?'

Dark colour had flushed his stunning cheekbones. 'I believed that you loved me, but I also knew that you had doubts and insecurities. Perhaps I expected too much from you.'

Sadness filled her. 'It was a big challenge to face leaving my family and everything I knew to live in a foreign country, but I would have done it to be with you. In hospital that morning I wondered if my illness was fate intervening, and I waited too long to ask Dad to give you a message. But if you'd come back, tried to see me or speak to me even…'

Valente grimaced. 'I'm obstinate. I'm very proud. At many times when my life has been difficult those were the strengths that carried me through,' he explained. 'But I should have had more faith in you. That is what finished us—my lack of faith. I was convinced you had wronged me, that your family had persuaded you to just leave me at the church. I blamed you for it all.'

Caroline wanted to cry. She wondered how she could have expected him to have faith in such circumstances, when so many people in his life had hurt him. 'I believed you had received my message before you went to the church. Matthew lied about that. He threw the truth at me after we were married, when he was annoyed with me, and admitted that he had made no attempt to get in touch with you.'

'As you learned too late, Matthew had a mean side,' Valente quipped.

'But you didn't?'

'No, I always had a ruthless streak,' Valente

contradicted. 'I wouldn't have survived or prospered in my world without it. The only person I ever allowed to see me without that armour was you.'

The tears overflowed from Caroline's eyes and rolled down her cheeks. Valente came down on the side of the bed and reached for her. She slapped away his hand in rejection. 'No, don't you dare touch me! How could you not read even one of my letters? How could you be dumb enough to see that as a test of how tough you could be?' she wailed at him furiously.

Valente gazed back at her with dark, strained eyes. 'It was that macho streak you don't like. You made me vulnerable and I didn't like it. This time around I wanted everything to be different.'

'And it certainly was that,' Caroline agreed, sliding off the far side of the bed and smoothing down her crumpled linen dress. 'You black-mailed me into bed with you.'

'And you blackmailed *me* into marriage,' Valente traded with amusement. 'Having worked out that I wanted you at any price, you then came up with the highest price you could think of. The biter was bitten.'

Caroline shifted uncomfortably. 'That wasn't how I saw it. I knew that once you found out I was frigid you'd ditch me and forget all your promises.'

Valente lifted a sardonic brow. 'Isn't it strange that I stuck by you instead of going for an annulment on the grounds of non-consummation?' he prompted. 'Why do you think that was?'

Caroline wore an uncertain look. 'Because you would have found that an embarrassing way to end our marriage?'

'My reputation is such that it would not have caused me embarrassment. I wanted more than your body, even if I wasn't prepared to admit that to myself at the time.'

'Well, you did a very good job of convincing me that all you wanted was sex,' Caroline told him, unimpressed.

Valente stood up. Lean, darkly handsome face intent, dark eyes brilliant, he strolled towards her. 'Don't you get the slightest vibe when a man loves you? You know I spent years plotting to get you back. You know I married you even though that wasn't part of my plan. You know I stayed with you even though it didn't immediately work out in the bedroom. Can't you see what all that has to add up to?'

'Are you trying to say that you love me—

even though you rejected *my* love?' Caroline shot at him in disbelief.

'I was doing that macho thing. But I've taken off the armour again. Tonight I finally appreciated that I love you more than anything in my life…even business,' Valente confided. 'And I know that's not a romantic comparison, but business is very important to me.'

'And I'm even more important?' Caroline felt out of breath, as though she had just run up a hill too fast.

'The very centre of my world, *cara mia*. Without you, my life would have no true meaning.'

Valente closed his arms round her slight figure with caution, for she was tense and wide-eyed, everything about her stance suggesting indecision. 'I held on to my memories of you long after I should have done, and unfortunately I held on to my bitterness as well. I love you very, very much,' he breathed softly. 'I was never able to forget you or replace you.'

Sheer excitement made her heart feel as if it was jumping for joy inside her chest. 'And you already know how I feel about you.'

'I didn't believe you when you said you loved me. I didn't believe you for a second,' Valente hastened to explain. 'I thought you were just using words to try and soften me up.'

As his beautiful, sensual mouth drifted downward in the direction of hers, Caroline took a hasty step back from him. 'I may love you, but that doesn't mean I can forgive you for setting up Bomark Logistics and blackmailing me into your bed.'

'Even though I promise that I will never do anything like that again?'

'Easy to say, when you know you don't need blackmail any more in the bedroom,' Caroline replied squarely.

'As proof of my good intentions, we could be celibate for a while,' Valente suggested silkily.

Caroline stiffened at that deeply unattractive prospect and, catching the raw gleam of mockery in his wicked gaze, was very nearly provoked into slapping him for his sense of humour. 'I think you know very well that you're in too much demand now to be required to make *that* sacrifice,' she said in a starchy tone.

'It would be a huge sacrifice,' Valente confessed, impelling her to him and then hoisting her slight body up against him with strong, impatient hands.

'Forget it, then.' She revelled in the driving

urgency of his kiss as though she had been waiting for it all her life. Her body came alive in his arms and hunger stirred in a hollow ache inside her pelvis. 'But how could you have dared to demand that I give you a child as well?'

'It gave me the best prospect of holding on to you long-term, *tesoro mia*,' Valente explained. 'I realised that if you were even half as fond of our baby as you are of your cat I would soon have you on a permanent basis, and that struck me as a very attractive option.'

Caroline studied him in dismay. 'You can be so calculating.'

Valente nodded confirmation, while easing her down on the bed and unzipping her dress in the process.

'It's shocking how much I love you...' Caroline whispered, feeling guilty at her lack of resistance.

His lean, darkly handsome features settled into a wolfish smile. 'Shock me all you like, *tesoro mia*. I will never stop loving you.'

'Nor I you.' And that was the most wonderful moment for Caroline, for she saw in the adoration in his gaze that he truly was as deeply attached to her as she was to him. For the first time in years she felt safe and secure and exactly where she belonged. Melting into his arms, she idly wondered if their baby—for she was convinced there would be one—would be dark or fair…

When he was born, eighteen months later, Pietro Lorenzatto took after his father in terms of build and features, and inherited his mother's pale blonde hair.

Isabel Hales peered down into the cot of her first grandson with admiring eyes, for Pietro was a very handsome baby. 'Women will go mad for him. Your son has got it all—the looks, the money, the background—'

'And a good healthy helping of his father's and his great-grandfather's lorry-driving genes!' Joe Hales teased, ambling cheerfully into the nursery to give his daughter a quiet hug. He touched the sparkling diamond pendant round her throat with a considering finger. 'You're looking well, Caro. I see Valente has been to the jewellers again. He must spend money as fast as he makes it.'

'Nonsense, Joe. He has an endless supply to spend.' Isabel moved closer, with the help of her walking frame, and studied her daughter with decided satisfaction. 'Valente knows how to treat Caroline. You've got a wonderful husband,' she pronounced, thoroughly impressed by her son-in-law's generosity. 'He loves buying you things.'

Caroline, svelte in the burgundy-coloured dress she had chosen to wear for the party about to be held in honour of her parents' fortieth wedding anniversary, simply smiled. She wondered what her mother would say if she was to learn that her daughter's most precious possession was not from her overflowing jewel box. It was a tiny Murano glass lucky black cat, given to her by Valente on the occasion of their son's birth. He had also given her a beautiful eternity ring, but the little glass cat, rousing memories as it did of that all-embracing first love which they had so magically contrived to recapture, held a much deeper significance for them both.

The party was being held that evening at Winterwood. Entertaining her friends there promised to give Isabel Hales her finest hour, for the old house was now an extremely impressive luxury home after its head-to toe makeover at her son-in-law's expense. Where once Caroline had winced at her mother's pronouncements, she now tended to look first at Valente, to check that he was managing to restrain his laughter—for, mercifully, Valente found her mother's airs and graces very funny.

Over the two years that had passed since their wedding, much had mellowed. Caroline still saw a lot of her parents—she flew over to England regularly for weekend visits, and flew her parents over to Tuscany for longer stays. Her father had made an excellent recovery and was a good deal fitter than he had been. Isabel Hales's mobility was still poor, but the addition of a lift to the main house and household help in their apartment had made a real improvement to the older woman's life and had enabled her to entertain her friends more often.

Koko had acquired a Siamese mate called Whisky, and now there were two cats in the workshop—two cats trying to sneak into the offices, and two cats to keep out of the bedroom. In an attempt to limit the invasion, Valente had said that under no circumstances was there to be any kittens, and Caroline, having won homeless Whisky his new home by telling Valente the most gigantic sob story on his behalf, had agreed. Koko, however, had begun to look a little chubby, and Caroline was now wondering how best to break the news to Valente that some very small kittens were on the way.

Hales and Bomark Logistics had merged on the Hales site, and there had been no job losses. Joe liked to drop in on Hales-Bomark Haulage, to take an unbiased look at the business operation there and report his findings back to Valente. Her husband had become part of the family in a way she had never dreamt he might, and that meant a great deal to her.

As her parents went down in the lift, to await the arrival of their first guests, Caroline dealt her a sleeping son a last loving smile. She had had an easy pregnancy and birth, and Pietro had slotted into their lives as though he had always been there. Their child had greatly added to their happiness. Shortly before her son was born Caroline's jewellery had won a design award, and she had garnered so many new customers from that publicity that she had had to expand her business. Now she did more designing than making, and found it easier to take time off.

She returned to the master bedroom to see if Valente, who had flown in late to attend the party, was changed yet.

Raking a comb through his luxuriant hair, and cursing the curls trying to spring up, Valente, supremely elegant in his dinner jacket, swung round from the mirror to look at her. An appreciative glow lightened his dark eyes to gold.

'You look amazing in that colour, but my favourite is still your wedding dress,' he admitted reflectively. 'I can't believe that we'll have been married two years next month, *tesoro mio*.'

Caroline folded into his extended arms like a homing pigeon coming back to roost. 'Mmm,' she sighed, loving the feel of him against her. 'I'm looking forward to the masked ball.'

'I hate fancy dress,' Valente groaned.

'You're going to look terrifically sexy, dressed up like one of your ancestors,' Caroline forecast—for the design of their outfits had been based on a couple of the Barbieri family portraits which she had chosen.

Valente stared down at her heart-shaped face, his gaze roving over its delicate loveliness with warm appreciation. He knew he would wreck her make-up if he succumbed to temptation and kissed her. He knew he was going to do it anyway.

Drawn by the same unbearably strong desire to feel his mouth on hers, Caroline gripped the lapels of his jacket and stretched up, and he took that encouragement with alacrity. He kissed her with passionate intensity. 'Three days without you can feel like a month, *tesora mia*,' Valente confessed.

'I missed you too…' Caroline locked her arms round him, their bodies straining together and taut with longing.

A faint shudder racked his lean, powerful length as she squirmed against him. 'Enough to be late for the party?'

'No, we couldn't,' she gasped, fighting the excitement rippling through her as he trailed his fingers up her thigh, lifting her skirt out of his path.

But Valente had heard that before, and he was not easily sidetracked. Persistence ensured that temptation triumphed, and when, some time later, the loving couple scrambled back into their discarded clothes, neither was quite as immaculate in appearance as before.

It was as Valente and a dreamy-eyed Caroline were descending the stairs to the party that Caroline took a deep breath and said, 'I've been meaning to tell you for a while…Koko's pregnant—there are kittens on the way. I thought when they grow up they could live at the villa…'

Valente sent his wife a highly amused appraisal. 'You picked the optimum moment to tell me. You have perfect timing, *tesora mia*.'

Caroline smiled and squeezed his hand, her heart so full of happiness she could hardly speak...

* * * * *

*Harlequin offers a romance for every mood!
See below for a sneak peek from our
suspense romance line
Silhouette® Romantic Suspense.
Introducing HER HERO IN HIDING by*
New York Times *bestselling author*
Rachel Lee.

Kay Young returned to woozy consciousness to find that she was lying on a soft sofa beneath a heap of quilts near a cheerfully burning fire. When she tried to move, however, everything hurt, and she groaned.

At once she heard a sound, then a stranger with a hard, harsh face was squatting beside her. "Shh," he said softly. "You're safe here. I promise."

"I have to go," she said weakly, struggling against pain. "He'll find me. He can't find me."

"Easy, lady," he said quietly. "You're hurt. No one's going to find you here."

"He will," she said desperately, terror clutching at her insides. "He always finds me!"

"Easy," he said again. "There's a blizzard outside. No one's getting here tonight, not even the doctor. I know, because I tried."

"Doctor? I don't need a doctor! I've got to get away."

"There's nowhere to go tonight," he said levelly. "And if I thought you could stand, I'd take you to a window and show you."

But even as she tried once more to pull away the quilts, she remembered something else: this man had been gentle when he'd found her beside the road, even when she had kicked and clawed. He hadn't hurt her.

Terror receded just a bit. She looked at him and detected signs of true concern there.

The terror eased another notch and she let her head sag on the pillow. "He always finds me," she whispered.

"Not here. Not tonight. That much I can guarantee."

Will Kay's mysterious rescuer protect her
from her worst fears?
Find out in HER HERO IN HIDING
by New York Times *bestselling author*
Rachel Lee.
Available June 2010,
only from Silhouette® Romantic Suspense.

Copyright © 2010 by Susan Civil-Brown

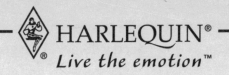

HARLEQUIN®
Live the emotion™

The series you love are now available in

LARGER PRINT!

The books are complete and unabridged—
printed in a larger type size to make it
easier on your eyes.

HARLEQUIN®
Romance

From the Heart, For the Heart

HARLEQUIN®

INTRIGUE®

Breathtaking Romantic Suspense

HARLEQUIN®
Presents®

Seduction and Passion Guaranteed!

HARLEQUIN®
Super Romance®

Exciting, Emotional, Unexpected

Try **LARGER PRINT** today!
Visit: www.eHarlequin.com
Call: 1-800-873-8635

LPDIR09

HARLEQUIN® *Romance*®

The rush of falling in love

Cosmopolitan
international settings

Believable, feel-good stories
about today's women

The compelling thrill
of romantic excitement

It could happen to you!

EXPERIENCE
HARLEQUIN ROMANCE!

Available wherever Harlequin books are sold.

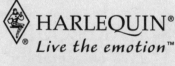

HARLEQUIN®
Live the emotion™

www.eHarlequin.com

HROMDIR09

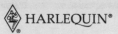

HARLEQUIN®

Invites *you* to experience lively, heartwarming all-American romances

Every month, we bring you four strong, sexy men, and four women who know what they want—and go all out to get it.

From small towns to big cities, experience a sense of adventure, romance and family spirit—the all-American way!

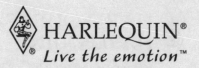

Love, Home & Happiness

HARLEQUIN®
Live the emotion™

www.eHarlequin.com

HARDIR09

HARLEQUIN®
INTRIGUE®

BREATHTAKING ROMANTIC SUSPENSE

Shared dangers and passions lead to electrifying
romance and heart-stopping suspense!

Every month, you'll meet six new heroes
who are guaranteed to make your spine tingle
and your pulse pound. With them you'll enter
into the exciting world of Harlequin Intrigue—
where your life is on the line
and so is your heart!

THAT'S INTRIGUE—
ROMANTIC SUSPENSE
AT ITS BEST!

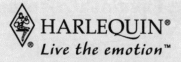

HARLEQUIN®
® *Live the emotion*™

www.eHarlequin.com   INTDIR06

...there's more to the story!

Superromance.
A *big* satisfying read about unforgettable
characters. Each month we offer *six* very different
stories that range from family drama to adventure
and mystery, from highly emotional stories to
romantic comedies—and much more! Stories
about people you'll believe in and care about.
Stories too compelling to put down....

Our authors are among today's *best* romance
writers. You'll find familiar names and talented
newcomers. Many of them are award winners—
and you'll see why!

If you want the biggest and best
in romance fiction, you'll get it
from Superromance!

Exciting, Emotional, Unexpected...

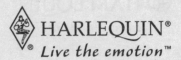

Live the emotion™

www.eHarlequin.com   HSDIR06